THE GUNSMITH

491

Invitation to a Bank Robbery

Books by J.R. Roberts
(Robert J. Randisi)

The Gunsmith series

Gunsmith Giant series

Lady Gunsmith series

Angel Eyes series

Tracker series

Mountain Jack Pike series

COMING SOON!
The Gunsmith
492 – A Fortune for the Gunsmith

For more information
visit: www.SpeakingVolumes.us

THE GUNSMITH

491

Invitation to a Bank Robbery

J.R. Roberts

SPEAKING VOLUMES, LLC
NAPLES, FLORIDA
2024

Invitation to a Bank Robbery

ISBN 979-8-89022-193-3

Chapter One

Clint Adams was tired.

He rode into Kennelworth, Utah feeling every mile that he had ridden over the past few days in his body. Even his Tobiano was carrying his head low. He rode down the main street without attracting any undue amount of attention. That suited him, since he was still looking for a place to rest. Recently, he thought he had found a place, but each time he got himself involved in someone's trouble—.

This time he was bound and determined to keep to himself, but on the other hand, who was he kidding? Why could he never let people handle their own problems? Especially ladies in distress. Having read stories about the knights of the legendary round table in King Arthur's Court, he wondered if he would have been a white knight back then, drawn in to play the hero against his will.

The main street of Kennelworth seemed to be crowded with shops, cafés and saloons. At one point, while riding past a lady's apparel shop he saw a tall raven-haired woman coming out, and noticed the purple gloves on her hands. For a moment their eyes met, before she turned her attention to the packages she was balancing in her arms. A pretty young girl, seated in a buggy stepped down and hurried to assist her. Several men passed by without offering to help. In fact, they seemed to cringe away from her.

Clint rode on until he came to a livery stable. The sound of metal-on-metal emanated from inside. He assumed a blacksmith was hammering out some horseshoes. He dismounted and walked the Tobiano inside. A large man with biceps like cannonballs paused in his hammering.

"Help ya?" the man asked.

"I just rode in and I'm looking for a place to board my horse."

"That's a fine animal," the man said. "I'd be happy to board him here. He looks in need of rest."

"And feed," Clint said.

"I'll take good care of him." He took the reins from Clint. "How long will you be stayin'?"

"I'm pretty tired, myself, so perhaps a few days. It looks like a good-sized town with a few saloons."

"We have half-a-dozen saloons, all with gambling."

"Sounds good." He grabbed his rifle and saddlebags. "I'll go and find lodging for myself, now."

"Try The Cattlemen's House."

"I think I passed the place when I rode in," Clint said. "It's a good one?"

"Not the best place in town, but it has one thing going for it."

"What's that?"

"It's not owned by Minerva Dawson."

"Who's she?"

"A local businesswoman," the man said. "She owns many businesses in town and runs them with an iron hand. There aren't a lot of people here who like her."

"I saw a woman as I was riding into town," Clint said. "Tall, dark-haired, she was wearing purple gloves."

"That's her," the man said. "She always wears those purple gloves."

"That's interesting," Clint said, "but I don't have any reason to get involved with her. I'll just go and check into the Cattleman's House and get a meal."

"They have a pretty good dining room."

"What's your name?"

"Finch."

"Thanks, Finch."

As Clint started to walk out Finch said, "Hey!"

Clint turned.

"What's *your* name?" Finch asked.

"I'm Clint, and that's Toby."

Finch stroked the Tobiano's nose and said, "Hiya, Toby."

Clint left and headed for the hotel.

***

Clint had never spent a very long period of time in Utah, but towns like Kennelworth were a dime a dozen. There were usually businessmen and women who owned multiple businesses, making friends and enemies while running them. Minerva Dawson didn't seem to be any different.

He had an edible steak in the hotel dining room after leaving his belongings in his room, which was clean.

"Anythin' else, sir?"

"No, thank you. That was enough."

He stood up and walked out to the lobby. He decided to walk around Kennelworth and see if he could find anything different about it.

Chapter Two

After a few hours Clint determined that the town wasn't much different from others. There were many thriving businesses, and some that were boarded up. He stepped into a doorway to read a sign that was posted on the wall. It announced that a leather shop would soon be opening, owned by Minerva Dawson. Seemed the lady was still expanding her empire.

He backed out of the doorway and two men ran right into him.

"Hey, watch it, friend!" one of them snapped.

Clint turned to face the men. They looked like visiting cowhands, except that they wore guns. The one with the big mouth was younger than the other.

"You stumbled into me, friend," Clint said to the young one. "Let's just call it an accident and part ways."

"How do you like that, Ed?" the young man asked. "He says we bumped into *him*."

"Have you been drinking this early?" Clint asked.

"Come on, Jack," the older man said. "He's right, we did run into him. Sorry, Mister. He's young."

"That's all right," Clint said. "Forget it. In the future try not to start drinking so early."

"Hey, look, friend—"

Ed grabbed Jack's arm. "Shut up, Jack. Let's move."

The older man, Ed, pushed Jack ahead of him. Clint watched them stumble down the street. This was just what he didn't need, trouble.

Normally, when arriving in a town, Clint would stop in the local sheriff or marshal's office and check in, assure the law he wasn't looking for trouble. This time, however, he figured to keep to himself until the time came when he had no choice but to talk to the law. And bumping into a couple of drunks didn't qualify.

He started walking again, stopped when he came to a small saloon called The Black & White Saloon. From what Finch told him about the lady with the purple gloves, he doubted this place belonged to Minerva Dawson.

He went inside and found it almost deserted. There was a bartender behind the bar, and two men seated at a table.

"Come on in, friend," the barkeep said. "Whataya have?"

"A cold beer, if you've got it."

"Comin' up."

The bartender, a big man with large hands, set a frothy beer down in front of Clint. He picked it up and drained half of it.

"You musta just rode in," the bartender said, "Come a long way?"

"I've been on the trail a while," Clint admitted. "I checked into the Cattleman's House and had a meal, then came looking for this." He raised his beer.

"First one's on the house, then," the barkeep said.

"Much obliged," Clint said. He finished the beer and put the mug down. "I'll pay for the second, gladly."

The bartender nodded and laughed. He drew the second and set it down.

"Thanks." Clint sipped it. "Is business always this light?"

"There are half a dozen saloons in town," the man said. "We're the smallest."

"I heard something about a lady named Dawson," Clint said. "A savvy businesswoman. I assume she doesn't own this place."

"You got that right," the bartender said. "But she owns three of the other saloons."

"So does your business ever get better than this?"

"Some nights we get a few cowhands from neighboring ranches," the bartender said.

"This seems like a nice quiet town."

"It used to be a lively place," the bartender said, "but things have changed. Are you lookin' to stay a while?"

"Long enough for me and my horse to get some rest," Clint said. "Tell me, what changed the town? You got a good lawman?"

"Fair to middlin'," the bartender said. "No, the thing that changed this town was the arrival of Minerva Dawson."

"And how long ago was that?"

"About five years," the bartender said. "She came to town with sacks of money and started buying up properties."

"She sounds like a tough, determined lady."

"That she is."

"You own this place?"

"I do," the man said, extending his hand. "The name's Byron."

They shook hands.

"I'm Clint." He finished his second beer. "Tell me, if she offered to buy this place, would you sell?"

"Not a chance," Byron said. "This is my place and it always will be."

"Then while I'm here in Kennelworth, this will be my place of comfort."

"You're welcome here, Clint. You can drink and— when it's available—gamble here."

"Thanks, Byron. I'll come back tonight."

"See ya then, Clint."

Clint left the Black & White Saloon.

Chapter Three

Clint had successfully found a place to sleep, and to drink. But his meal, while edible, was not satisfactory, so he still needed to find a better café. He decided to return to the livery stable and see what Finch had to say.

"Back so soon? Your horse is in my most comfortable stall," the big man said.

"Thanks," Clint said, "but I'm here to ask you to recommend a good place to eat."

"Didn't you have something at your hotel?"

"I did, but I'm looking for a good meal."

"There's a place on the corner of Main Street and Fourth," Finch said. "It's called The Bellflower Café."

"The Bellflower. Thanks, Finch."

"And if you want a place to drink, try The Black & White Saloon."

"I've already been there."

"Then you met Byron."

"I did," Clint said.

Finch smiled. "He's my cousin."

"He's even bigger than you are," Clint observed.

"He's my older cousin," Finch said. "I'll see you there tonight."

"I'll see you there."

Clint left the stable and walked to the café on the corner of Main and Fourth Streets. There was a large window in front with the name painted on it, and inside were blue curtains that were drawn.

He entered the café and was met at the door by a man in a white apron.

"Would you like a table, Sir?"

"Yes, I would. One in the back, please."

"Certainly. Follow me, please."

Clint had been in many cafés in many towns. This one was among the most beautifully decorated in reds and greens. The odors emanating from the kitchen were making him drool. They walked past other occupied tables with people eating chicken and steaks, stews and soups.

"Is this table satisfactory, Sir?" the waiter asked.

"It's fine."

"Would you like to see a menu?"

"Is there a special?"

"Yes, sir, a wonderful beef stew."

"I'll have that, then."

"Coming up. And to drink?"

"Coffee, black and strong."

"Right away."

The waiter went through a door Clint assumed led to the kitchen. The other diners in the room paid no attention to him.

The waiter soon returned with a pot of coffee, poured a cup, then returned to the kitchen. When he came back he was carrying a steaming bowl.

"Enjoy," he said, setting it down. "I'll bring you some bread."

"Thank you."

By the time the bread came Clint had sampled the stew and found it delicious. He finished it and sopped up the gravy with the bread.

"Anything else, sir?" the waiter asked.

"No," Clint said, "that was fine."

"Very well." The waiter handed Clint a bill, which he paid before leaving.

He was satisfied with what he had accomplished for the day. The Tobiano was being cared for, and he had a meal and a room. He decided to go to his room for a while, before returning to the Black & White Saloon for some distraction.

***

When he entered the saloon later that evening there were only a few more customers than the last time.

"You're back," Byron said.

"I told your cousin Finch I'd meet him here."

"He'll be along," Byron said. "A beer while you wait?"

"Sure."

Byron set a cold beer on the bar. Clint picked it up and looked around.

"Are these regular customers?"

"As regular as I get," Byron said. "A poker game might start soon, if you're interested."

"Not tonight, but thanks. I'll keep it in mind for the rest of the time I'm here."

"I'm sorry, I don't have any girls workin' for me, these days," Byron said.

"That's okay," Clint said. "I can usually find my own girls."

"We have a whorehouse in town," Byron offered.

"Nope," Clint said. "I never pay."

"Really?"

"There's too much out there for free," Clint explained.

"Maybe for a man like you," Byron said. "Not for a big lug like me. I like whores."

"A lot of men do," Clint said. "And there's nothing wrong with that."

"There's Finch," Byron said, as the big hostler came through the batwing doors.

Chapter Four

Byron had a beer on the bar for his cousin by the time Finch reached them.

"I been lookin' forward to this all day," Finch said, picking the mug up and draining it.

Byron quickly set down another one.

"What were you fellas talkin' about when I came in?" Finch asked.

"Whores," Byron said. "Clint says he don't like 'em."

"Whataya got against whores?" Finch asked.

"Nothing," Clint said. "Some of the nicest people I know are whores. I just don't pay for sex."

"Sure, you don't have to," Finch said. "That's for us ugly types."

"Big and ugly," Byron said, and he and his cousin laughed.

Clint finished his beer and set the empty mug down.

"Doesn't look like there's much going on here tonight," he said. "I'm going back to my hotel. I'll see you fellas tomorrow."

"G'night, Clint," Finch said.

As Clint left he heard Finch asking his cousin for another beer.

***

Clint read some Poe before turning in. In the morning, he went back to the Bellflower Café for breakfast. The waiter greeted him at the door. He looked older this morning than Clint remembered, in his thirties.

"You can sit anywhere," the waiter said. "We're not busy in the mornin'."

"I'll still take a back table," Clint said.

"Any one you like. I'll get you some coffee."

"And I'll take steak-and-eggs."

"Comin' up."

"What's your name?" Clint asked.

"I'm Ted Cory. My wife, Lily, is the cook. I'll be right back."

The waiter brought the coffee, then the steak-and-eggs.

"This is good," Clint said, after one bite. "Why don't you do any business at breakfast?"

"Most of the people in town eat breakfast at Minerva's," the man said.

"Minerva Dawson's place?"

"One of them," he said. "We get some lunch and dinner customers."

"Is her food as good as yours?"

"No," the waiter said, "my wife's the best cook in town."

"Has Miss Dawson tried to hire her?"

"Several times," the waiter said. "She offers more money each time."

"Is she eventually going to find your wife's price?" Clint asked.

"I hope not. I'll get you a basket of hot biscuits."

"Sounds good."

Clint attacked his breakfast, found himself thinking curiously about Minerva Dawson. He started to think that maybe he would like to meet her.

Ted came back with the biscuits.

"I've been told Miss Dawson rules her businesses with an iron fist."

"That's right," Ted said, "an iron fist in a purple velvet glove."

"What's the thing with the gloves?"

Ted shrugged.

"The lady likes gloves."

"What does she use to get her way?" Clint asked. "Does she employ some hard men?"

"She's a hard lady," Ted said. "She handles things herself."

"No employees?"

"Oh sure," Ted said, "she's got people workin' for her, running her businesses, but when somebody rubs her the wrong way, she handles it herself."

"How?" Clint asked. "Does she use a gun?"

"She uses whatever will do the trick," Ted said. "If somebody needs to be shot she'll do it herself."

"What's the sheriff do about that?"

Ted laughed.

"He doesn't do a damn thing. He's afraid of her."

"She scares the law?" Clint asked.

"She scares everybody."

Clint put his utensils down and sat back in his chair.

"I've got to admit," Clint said, "she sounds like a lady I'd like to meet. Where does she hang her hat?"

"She has rooms above The Purple Heart Saloon."

"Purple?"

"It's her color."

"What's the sheriff's name?"

"Frank Sills."

"What's he like?" Clint asked.

"Not a bad lawman, as long as he doesn't have to deal with Minerva."

"Been sheriff long?"

"About five years."

"Minerva got here five years ago, didn't she?" Clint asked.

"That's right."

"Maybe I'll stop in and see him first."

Chapter Five

As he walked to the sheriff's office, Clint had to admit his curiosity about the lady with the purple gloves was getting the best of him. When he reached the office he knocked and entered.

A man in his fifties sat at a desk that faced the door, so he just looked up at Clint.

"Can I help you?" he asked.

"I arrived in town yesterday, Sheriff," Clint said. "I just thought it would be a good idea if I checked in with you."

"Is that right? Why?"

"I'd like to avoid any trouble."

"What makes you think you'd run into trouble?" the lawman asked. "Who are you?"

"My name's Clint Adams."

Sheriff Sills froze for a moment, then asked, "The Gunsmith?"

"That's right."

The man sat back in his chair and took a deep breath before speaking again.

"I reckon I can see how you might expect trouble," he said. "If somebody should recognize you . . ."

". . . I'd still do what I could to avoid trouble."

"That's good news," Sills said. "This is a quiet little town."

"So I've heard," Clint said. "I'm going to walk around a bit, see what I can see. Just tell me if you've got any would be gunnies in town."

"Not that I know of."

"I bumped into two men named Jack and Ed yesterday," Clint said. "Jack was a hot head. Ed seemed to be able to control him."

"They're a couple of Bar-H hands. Jack's harmless as long as he's with Ed."

"And who else in town is . . . interesting?" Clint asked.

Sheriff Sills studied him for a moment, then said, "You've obviously heard some stories."

"One or two."

"About Minerva Dawson?"

"Yes. I'm curious about her."

"If you're really serious about avoiding trouble," the lawman said, "you'll avoid Minerva."

"Well," Clint said, "I stopped in your town to relax, and rest my horse."

"You're welcome to do that," Sills said. "But remember what I said about Minerva."

"Thanks for the advice, Sheriff."

Clint left the office.

***

Clint knew the sheriff's advice was good. He was looking to avoid trouble and get some rest. Why was he letting Minerva Dawson interest him so much? He was a victim of his own curiosity.

The Purple Heart Saloon was easy to find, as it had a large purple heart over the entrance. But it was early and the door was still locked. He kept walking, figuring he would return later.

He had been in town less than a full day and figured he had already made three friends: Finch, Byron and Ted. What he knew about Minerva Dawson he had learned from them, and from Sheriff Sills. Maybe he would be wise to just leave it at that. After all, his intention was to try and change his ways, and stay out of other people's affairs. If this town didn't mind being under Minerva Dawson's purple thumb, why should he care?

***

Jack Eads and Ed Gregory rode into town early, having been given a couple of days off from the Bar-H. The saloons were not yet open, so they chose to get a table at the Butterworth Café, which was mostly empty.

They ordered ham-and-eggs and coffee and waited-but Jake was waiting impatiently.

"Ed," the teenty-five-year-old said, "I'm gettin' tired of punchin' cows. There just ain't no money in it."

"Then what do you want to do?" the forty year old asked.

"This here is a quiet town," Jack said. "And it ain't got much of a lawman."

"So?"

"It's got a bank."

"Jack—"

"No, just listen," Jack said. "I've looked it over and it would be an easy job."

Ed leaned forward and hissed, "Rob a bank? Are you crazy?"

"No, I ain't," Jack said. "I'm tired of punchin' cows."

"So quit and move on."

"That's what I intend to do with the bank money," Jack said.

"So why are you tellin' me?"

"I need your help," Jack said. "It's an easy job, but it needs two men."

"You know Dawson's money is in that bank," Ed said.

"So what? We grab the cash and ride out of town. We'll be gone before she knows what happened. Come on, don't tell me you're afraid of a woman."

"She ain't just a woman."

"Come on Ed," Jack said, "don't tell me you're happy punching cattle?"

"Have you ever robbed a bank before?" Ed asked.

"No," Jack said, "that's part of what makes it exciting."

"Let me look at the bank and think it over," Ed said. "We might want to bring somebody else in on it."

"Like who?" Jack asked. "There ain't nobody from the Bar-H I'd trust."

"Maybe a stranger in town who doesn't know anything about Minerva Dawson."

"Like who, that fella who ran into us yesterday?" Jack asked.

"You ran into him, you drunken sot!" Ed said.

"Why a stranger?" Jack asked, frowning.

"We could use somebody to take the blame," Ed said.

Jack brightened. "Oh, I get it. Everybody chases him while we make a getaway with the money."

"Exactly," Ed said.

"Ed," Jack said, "have you done this before?"

"Maybe once or twice," Ed admitted.

Chapter Six

Clint walked past two other saloons: The Chuckwagon and The Gold Mine. The doors were open, but he didn't go into either one. He decided to walk back to The Purple Heart. He just wanted to take a look at it.

As he entered through the batwing doors, he saw that even at this early hour, the place was doing a fine business. He wondered if all these people were drinking there because they were afraid not to. Minerva Dawson certainly had a heady reputation.

He walked to the bar and easily found a space for himself.

"Help ya?" the tall, lanky barman asked. He was in his forties, with dark hair that came to a sharp, widow's peak.

"A cold beer, please," Clint said.

"Comin' up."

While waiting for his beer Clint noticed he was attracting some attention from men at the bar, and at nearby tables. He wondered if Sheriff Sills had spread the word that the Gunsmith was in town.

"Here ya go. First time here?"

"Yep."

"First one's on the house, then."

"Thanks."

Holding his beer, Clint turned and leaned back against the bar. Purple was a predominant color in the dresses the saloon girls wore, and vests the various dealers sported. As well as various fixtures on the walls and the ceiling.

One of the girls, a pretty brunette, came over and stood next to him.

"New in town?"

"That's right."

"Want some company?"

"What's your name?" he asked.

"I'm Tammy."

"Well, Tammy, not right now. I'm just having a look around."

"But you'll come back later?"

"I will," Clint said, "unless I find someplace better."

"Oh, you won't," Tammy said. "Believe me. Miss Dawson owns some other saloons in town, but this is the best one."

"Then I'll be back."

"Maybe later tonight you could meet her," Tammy said. "She's a very impressive lady."

"That's what I've been hearing around town."

"Well," she said, "if you don't want any company right now, maybe you'd like to do some gambling."

"That's possible," he said. "I'll look around. Are the house games honest?"

Tammy laughed. "They better be, or they'll have to deal with Miss Dawson. I have to go back to work now. I'll see you later."

"Later, Tammy."

As Tammy walked away the bartender leaned over the bar.

"Pretty girl," he said.

"Yes, she is. And young."

"She might be young, but she's also very experienced."

"Well, I'm not looking for that kind of entertainment. Not just yet, anyway."

"Some of the other girls might be more to your liking," the bartender said. "Or maybe the whorehouse?"

"Definitely not the whorehouse."

"Too bad," the barman said. "It's a popular place."

Something occurred to Clint, then.

"Tell me something," Clint said, turning to face the man, "does Miss Dawson own the whorehouse, too?"

"She owns quite a few businesses in town," the man said. "Excuse me."

Clint noticed the man had been careful not to answer the question.

Chapter Seven

Clint walked around the room, spending some time watching the blackjack and faro tables. From what he could see, the dealers were honest enough.

He returned to the bar, still aware that he was being watched.

"Find any interestin' games?" the barman asked.

"They all look honest," Clint said.

"Are you an expert?"

"I know a bottom dealer when I see one."

"I guess you do," the bartender said.

"Do you know who I am?" Clint asked.

"I may have heard something about you bein' Clint Adams," the bartender said.

"The sheriff?"

"He might have said somethin'."

Clint looked up and down the bar.

"Do you think any of these fellas heard the gossip. Seems like they find me interesting."

"I haven't heard them say anythin'," the bartender said, "but some of them might know. Frank Sills likes to talk."

"What about Miss Dawson?" Clint asked. "Does she know?"

"That I can't say," the bartender said.

"Can't, or won't?"

"Can't," the bartender said. "She doesn't keep me informed. I'm just a bartender."

"I see."

"Another beer?"

"No, thanks. I'm going to get some lunch."

He walked to the batwing doors, feeling eyes on him. He was sure there were some men in the saloon who knew who he was. That was a chance he took when he told the sheriff his name.

For lunch he returned to The Bellflower Café. There were a few customers having lunch.

"I guess this makes you a regular," Ted said. "Sandwich, or somethin' hot?"

"Let's do a sandwich," Clint said. "And some coffee."

"Comin' up."

Clint settled comfortably into a chair at a back table and waited. Ted returned with a thick chicken sandwich and a pot of coffee.

"The word on you is out. People know the Gunsmith is in town. What they don't know is why."

"I'm not sure of that, myself," Clint said. "Originally it was just for a rest. Now my curiosity is getting the better of me."

"Curiosity about Minerva Dawson?"

"Yes."

"Have you met her, yet?"

"No, not yet. I did go to the Purple Heart to look it over. It's impressive."

"I suppose so."

"Have you been there?" Clint asked.

"No," Ted said, "I don't spend much time in any of the saloons."

"You don't drink?"

"I do, but at home, in the evenings," Ted said. "My wife and me, we share some brandy. Hey, enjoy your lunch. I've got a few more customers."

As Ted walked away Clint lifted the sandwich and bit into it. It was built of tender white meat, tomatoes, lettuce, on good homemade bread.

After several bites he washed them down with coffee, then took several more. He continued to eat that way until the sandwich was gone.

"More coffee?" Ted asked.

"No, thanks," Clint said. "That was an excellent sandwich."

"Everything my wife makes is excellent," Ted said.

***

Ed met Jack at the Gold Mine Saloon. He bought two beers at the bar and carried them to Jack's table.

"So?" Jack asked. "Did you look the bank over?"

"I did."

"And?"

"It's doable."

"I told you," Jack said. "When do we do it?"

"It needs to be planned, Jack," Ed said.

"What about that cowboy we ran into?" Jack said. "You were gonna recruit him."

"That's gonna be hard to do," Ed said.

"Why's that?"

Ed sipped his beer, then put it down.

"I found out who that stranger is," Ed said.

"Who is he?"

"Clint Adams."

Jack looked surprised.

"The Gunsmith? What's he doin' here?"

"Supposedly, he's just passin' through."

"But that's perfect."

"Whataya mean?"

"Don't you see?" Jack said. "We rob the bank, and the Gunsmith takes the blame."

Chapter Eight

Ed and Jack left The Gold Mine Saloon and walked to the sheriff's office. As they entered, Frank Sills turned from the potbellied stove, coffee pot in one hand, and mug in the other.

"What can I do for you boys?" he asked. "Coffee?"

"Not from your office pot, Frank," Ed said to his friend. "That stuff's poison."

Sills finished pouring and said, "I like my coffee." He put the pot back on top of the stove and walked to his desk. "What brings you here?"

"The Gunsmith," Ed said.

"Stay away from him, Ed," Sills said.

"We ain't afraid of him," Jack said.

"I can believe that of you, kid," Sills said. "You're a fool. But you, Ed. You're no fool."

"We have a plan, Frank," Ed said. "I wanna run it by you."

"A plan to do what?"

"To get us all enough money to get away from here," Ed said.

"Ed, Ed," Sills said, shaking his head, "what crazy idea has this kid put in your head."

"Hey—" Jack started, but Ed waved him off. "Look, Frank," he said, "I think we're all kind tired of livin' the way we are. Jack and me, we've got an idea."

"What is it?"

"Don't worry about that," Ed said. "First I wanna ask you about the Gunsmith."

"You're not gonna tangle with him, are you?"

"What's he doin' here?" Ed asked.

"He says he just stopped to rest."

"Do you believe him?"

Sills shrugged and asked, "Why not?"

"No, not him," Ed said. "A man like him's gotta be lookin' for somethin'."

"Like what?"

"That's what I wanna find out," Ed said. "Me and Jack, we think he'd be useful."

"Gettin' involved with him ain't a good idea, Ed."

"We'll see, Sheriff. We'll see."

Ed turned to leave, followed by Jack.

"Hey," Sills snapped, "ain't you gonna tell me this great idea you got?"

"You just stay ready," Ed said. "We'll bring you in when the time comes."

Outside they stopped.

"Whataya think, Ed?" Jack asked. "Will Sills throw in with us?"

"I think so," Ed said. "He's had enough of wearin' that badge."

"So we just need to get to the Gunsmith and see if he's available."

Ed turned and got face-to-face with the younger man.

"Jack, you stay away from him," Ed said, "Leave Clint Adams to me."

"When?" Jack asked. "When are you gonna approach him?"

"I'll talk to him tonight, just to get the feel of 'im."

"And what do I do, in the meantime?"

"Stay at the Gold Mine so I can find you," Ed said.

"And what about the Bar-H?" Jack asked. "We stay away too long we'll lose our jobs."

"If we pull this off," Ed said, "we won't need those jobs. Let's go see where the Gunsmith is."

They stepped off the boardwalk and crossed the street.

***

They walked along Main Street, looking in windows. They finally spotted Clint Adams sitting at a table in the Bellflower Café.

"Well, there he is," Jack said. "Let's go."

Ed put his hand on Jack's chest.

"You go on to the Gold Mine," he said, "I'll talk to Adams."

"Be convincin', Ed."

"I'll do my best."

Jack walked on, while Ed entered the café.

***

Clint saw the two men through the large front window. He watched them while he finished his lunch. He was pushing his plate away when the men separated. The young one walked away, and the older one entered the café. Ted greeted him, then turned and looked at Clint, who nodded.

"You mind if I join you?" Ed asked.

"Have a seat," Clint said. "Want some coffee?"

"Sure, thanks."

Clint turned over an extra mug and poured.

"What's on your mind?" Clint asked.

"My name's Ed Gregory," the man said. "My young friend is Jack Eads. We're cow punchers, but we've got an idea that will change that."

"Is that right?"

Ed nodded and said, "It is. And we think you can help us."

"Why don't you tell me about it, then?" Clint said.

Chapter Nine

"We want to rob the bank," Ed said.

"How many banks are in town?" Clint asked.

"Just the one."

"And how many of you are there?" Clint asked.

"Just me and Jack," Ed said. "And maybe you."

Clint laughed and sat back.

"You want me to help you rob the bank?"

"Why not?" Ed asked. "You're a stranger here. Why should a man with your reputation care if the bank is robbed?"

"There's never been anything in any description of my reputation that includes bank robbery."

"There's always a first time," Ed said. "I've cased the bank, and it should be very simple."

"What about the local law, Sheriff Sills?" Clint asked. "Do you think he'll stand by and watch?"

"Sheriff Sills won't be a problem," Ed said. "He's a friend of mine."

"So he's going along with this?"

"He doesn't know about it, yet," Ed said, "but he'll go along. There's enough money in the bank for all of us to live new lives."

If the local lawman was in on the plan, there was no harm in Ed approaching Clint about robbing the bank. Who could Clint tell that would take it upon themselves to stop it? And if Clint decided not to take part in the robbery, should he be the one to stop it? This wasn't his town. Why should he even get involved?

"I'll need more information before I can decide," Clint told Ed.

That response seemed to satisfy the man.

"I've still got a few things to iron out," Ed said. "I'll fill you in when we're ready to go."

"I'll be around," Clint said.

Ed stood up.

"This'll work out, Mr. Adams."

"We'll see," Clint said. "I'm still not sure about your young partner."

"Don't worry about Jack," Ed said. "He'll be solid."

"And your friend, the sheriff?"

"That's another thing," Ed said, "but I've got plans for him."

Clint was sure Ed had a lot of plans he was keeping to himself.

"I'll be in touch," Ed said.

"I'll be around."

Ed nodded and left. The other diners in the place paid no attention.

Clint felt he had been presented with an interesting dilemma. Turn the offer down and ignore the whole thing? Or do what he could to stop it? He certainly wasn't going to take part in the robbery, and he wondered what made Ed believe that he might?

Then he got an idea. He thought of somebody he could warn about the bank robbery, who would probably take action. And it would also satisfy his curiosity about Minerva Dawson. Surely she had a nice, tidy sum of money in the bank, and would not like to see anybody ride off with it.

Satisfied that he had come up with a solution, he left the café and headed for The Purple Heart Saloon.

***

It was afternoon, and people were drinking and gambling. He was sure by the time darkness fell, they would be packed in shoulder-to-shoulder. If her many other businesses were not making money, at least this place was a cash cow for her.

He went to the bar, where he had to shoulder his way in. The men he pushed his way between turned to look at him, seemed to recognize him, and moved aside willingly.

"Whataya have?" the bartender asked.

"A beer," Clint said, "and I'd like to see Miss Dawson."

The barkeep brought him his beer and said, "She don't see just anybody."

"If you tell her who I am I think she'll see me."

Clint waited for the bartender to ask who he was, but instead the man said, "Wait here."

The bartender made his way through the crush of people and disappeared. There was a staircase to the second floor, and Clint didn't see the man go up, so Dawson's office must have been downstairs.

"You're back!"

Clint turned his head and saw the saloon girl, Tammy standing there, smiling at him.

"I am," he agreed.

"Looking for me?"

"I'm afraid not yet," he said. "I'm here to see your boss."

"She's not here," Tammy said. "She went out a little while ago."

"Do you know where she went?"

"She said she was going to church," Tammy told him.

"Where is the church?"

"At the north end of town."

"Thanks, Tammy." He put his beer mug on the bar.

"You could wait for her here?"

"I'll see if I can catch her at the church," Clint said. "It'll be quieter. When the bartender comes back, tell him I left."

"Should I tell him where you went?" she asked.

"No harm done if you do," he said, and left the saloon.

Chapter Ten

Clint walked to the north end of town. As he approached he saw the cross atop a steeple. As he got closer he saw there was no activity. Thinking she was probably inside he started up the steps. But before he reached the door it opened and a woman wearing purple gloves, a purple jacket and skirt, stopped when she saw him.

"There's no service now," she told him.

"Then what were you doing in there?"

"I come here often, just to think," she said. "You're Clint Adams, aren't you?"

"I am."

"I saw you ride into to town yesterday," she said. "What are you doing here?"

"Actually, I was looking for you."

"How did you know where I was?"

"I went to The Purple Heart, and they told me you came here. I hope you don't mind, but it would be much quieter to talk here."

"Talk about what?"

"Just some news I thought might interest you. Can we go somewhere?"

"Inside," she said. "There's no one there."

"No pastor?"

"We haven't had a pastor for quite some time. Shall we go in?"

Clint came up the steps the rest of the way and entered the church with Minerva Dawson.

She led the way down the center aisle to the first row and sat.

"Join me," she said. It came out more of an order than invitation.

Clint sat in the same row, leaving a space between them. He studied her for a moment, found her a mature woman of some beauty. She was probably on the plus side of forty.

"I know your reputation, Mr. Adams," she said. "What's on your mind?"

"I understand you pretty much own this town."

"I don't own the town, but I do own a good portion of it. Are you looking for a job?"

"No, just the opposite. I've been offered one."

"Oh? And why would that interest me?"

"It's the bank, Miss Dawson," Clint said. "I've been approached to assist in robbing it."

"Oh? Is that the kind of thing you do?"

"Not at all," Clint said. "If I was going to take the job, I wouldn't be warning you. After all, I assume you have an account there."

"Oh yes, a personal one and a business one. Tell me, who offered you this job?"

"A man named Ed Gregory," Clint said. "He and his friend, Jack, are cowhands at one of the ranches around here."

"What are you going to do?" she asked.

"I told Ed I'd think about it."

"Are you going to go to the sheriff?"

"According to Ed, the sheriff's a friend of his and is going to take part in the robbery."

"So your next thought was to come to me?"

"I couldn't think of anyone else," Clint said. "Since you seem to be so feared in this town, I thought you'd know what to do."

"Yes, right, of course," she said. "I do know what to do."

"And what's that?"

"If the sheriff is in on it, I'll need to hire someone to prevent the robbery . . ."

"Now, wait—"

"That would be you," she finished.

"I really don't want to get that involved," he said.

"What else were you planning to do?"

"I was going to meet with Ed and tell him to get somebody else."

"Don't you think he'd kill you rather than let you walk away?" she asked.

"He'd probably try."

"Then I don't even need to hire you," she said. "Some cowpoke and would-be bank robber wouldn't have a chance against you."

"You're probably right."

"So you'll put a stop to this plan?"

"Miss Dawson—"

"Minerva, please."

"Minerva, I try my best to avoid trouble."

"You strike me as the kind of man who can't avoid trouble," she said. "After all, you weren't asking for this invitation to a bank robbery, yet here we are. How can you avoid stopping it? I can make it easy for you, though. I can pay you."

"I'm not looking for any money," he said, "from you or the bank robbers."

"Very well, then," she said. "You've told me about it. Your next move would be to tell Ed you won't help. After that we'll just have to see what happens."

"Don't you have some men you could send after Ed and Jack? And maybe to guard the bank."

"I don't keep hired gunmen on my payroll," she said.

"What if you run into trouble?"

"I tend to handle it myself."

"So if I walk out of here, get on my horse and ride, what will you do?"

"I'd have to find this Ed and Jack and take care of them myself."

"With what?"

"I have a gun" she said. "I don't wear it, but I know how to use it."

"And you'd go up against two men?"

"Two cowboys," she said. "Even if they rob the bank, they're not gunmen."

They both fell silent for a moment, alone with their thoughts.

"Well," she said, then, "are you leaving town?"

"Not just yet."

"Then I'll wait to hear from you on whether or not I need to handle this myself."

She stood up.

"Tell me something," he said.

"What's that?"

"What's with the purple gloves?"

She shrugged and said, "I like purple."

Chapter Eleven

Minerva refused Clint's offer to walk her back to The Purple Heart.

"Folks in this town are used to seeing me walk alone," she told him. "I don't want to change their impression of me."

"If you say so."

"You go and find your man and tell him your decision. Let's see what happens."

"I know what you want to happen, but I don't think he'll try to kill me right off."

"Either way, let me know," she said. "I'll be waiting at The Purple Heart and thank you, Mr. Adams, for the warning," she said. "Rest assured if you don't stop them, I'll take some action."

"I might be interested in seeing that."

"I'll try not to disappoint you."

He watched her walk away until she was out of sight. Along the way townspeople stepped aside.

Clint assumed that after leaving the café Ed would have gone somewhere to meet up with Jack. But where? Probably another saloon. They wouldn't be going back to the Bar-H. They wouldn't think they needed their jobs anymore after robbing the bank.

Clint decided to check the other saloons in town for Ed and Jack.

***

Minerva Dawson entered The Purple Heart Saloon. As she did, she exchanged a look with the bartender, then crossed the room to the stairs. Along the way men watched her, but none spoke to her or made any advance. She went up the stairs, while the bartender looked for someone to spell him. When he had a man firmly entrenched behind the bar, he followed Minerva Dawson up the stairs. He knocked on her door.

"Come in, Ken."

He opened the door, entered and closed it behind him.

"Did the Gunsmith find you?" he asked.

"He did. Was it you who told him where I was?"

"No, it was Tammy."

"I'll have to have a talk with her," Minerva said. She had already undressed and put on a silk robe—a purple one, of course.

"What did he want?" Ken asked.

"He told me someone approached him about helping to rob the bank."

"What? When? Is he gonna do it?"

"He has no intention of robbing our bank," she said. "In fact, I'm hoping he'll take steps to stop it."

"Who approached him?"

"Some cowpoke who's decided to become a bank robber," she said. "He and his friend. Their names are Ed and Jack. Do you know anyone by those names?"

"Can't say I do. What about the sheriff?"

"You know Sills isn't any good," she said. "And this Ed told Adams the sheriff was a friend of his."

"So he'll be in on it?"

"Apparently."

"And Adams will go up against them alone?"

"I don't know," she said. "He's going to tell Ed he decided not to do it."

"This fella might try to kill him, then," Ken said.

"I hope he does," Minerva said. "Try, I mean. Then Adams will kill him, and this will be over."

"When?"

"He said he'll let me know what happens. I just wanted you to know. Next time he comes in, let him come up."

"I will."

"You can go back down now, Ken," she said. "And do me a favor. Send Tammy up."

He opened the door, then turned and asked, "Are you gonna fire her?"

"No," Minerva said, "just give her a talking to."

"Good," he said. "She's just a kid."

He left, closing the door behind him.

Chapter Twelve

Clint found Ed and Jack in The Gold Mine Saloon. He watched for a short time, to make sure it was just the two of them he would have to deal with. The saloon was crowded, but they sat at their table alone.

He entered the saloon and made his way across the floor, through the crowd, to their table.

"Mind if I join you?" he asked.

Both cowpokes looked up at him in surprise.

"Sure, why not?" Ed said.

Clint pulled out a chair and sat between them at an angle so he could watch the room.

Ed and Jack each had a beer mug in front of them.

"Want a beer?" Ed asked.

"No, thanks," Clint said. "I won't be here that long."

"What's on your mind?" Ed asked.

"The offer you made me," Clint said. "I'm going to have to turn you down."

"I'm sorry to hear that," Ed said. "Do you mind tellin' me why?"

"I've been on the right side of the law my whole life," Clint said. "I don't think I want to change sides just now."

"You're turnin' down a lot of money," Jack said.

"That may be, but that's my decision."

"So if you're not gonna help us, are you gonna try to stop us?"

"I'd like to say I'm just going to mind my own business," Clint replied, "but I can't. I'm afraid I'd have to stop you."

"Turn us is?" Ed asked.

"I wouldn't know who to turn you in to," Clint said. "You told me the sheriff's with you."

"That's true," Ed said. "But you could send for outside help. Maybe a federal marshal?"

Clint shook his head.

"I doubt I'd get anyone here in time," Clint said. "Although I don't know your timetable."

"Let's just assume you don't have time," Ed said.

"Well, there you go, then," Clint said. "I can only hope I can convince you to abandon your plan."

"No way," Jack said.

Clint looked at the young man.

"I figured *you'd* say that."

"This whole thing was my idea, Adams," Jack said. "I'm not about to change my mind."

"Have you ever robbed a bank before?" Clint asked.

"No," Jack said, "but Ed has."

Clint looked at Ed.

"I haven't always been punchin' cows."

"I see."

"Well," Ed said, "I hope you'll decide to not stand in our way."

"I'll stop you if I can, Ed."

"I don't see why," Ed said. "Yeah, okay, you don't wanna rob a bank, but what do you care if we do? You don't owe this town nothin'."

"That's true, but I can't just stand by when I know about it. And if you happen to kill somebody—"

"We don't intend to kill nobody," Ed said. "It's gonna be simple."

Clint looked at Jack. He doubted anything would be easy with a hothead like him involved.

"Is that all?" Ed asked. "Did you expect me to go for my gun when you turned me down?"

"To tell you the truth, I had no idea how you'd react," Clint said.

"I'm not a hothead, Adams," Ed said. "I've been around for a while."

"I guess so."

"Let's just agree that we couldn't do business, and leave it at that," Ed suggested.

"That suits me," Clint said, but he hesitated to stand.

"Don't worry," Ed said, "neither one of us wants to try your gun."

Clint wasn't so sure when it came to Jack. The younger man looked like he was itching for a fight.

"You keep young Jack, here, in his seat, and his hand away from his gun, and we should be fine."

"Jack's not gonna do anythin' stupid," Ed said. "At least, not just yet. You got my solemn word on that."

Clint stood up and melded into the crowd on his way to the door. He didn't think there was any way Ed and Jack would start shooting in there.

***

"You shoulda let me try him," Jack said.

"He would've shot you dead, Jack," Ed said. "You're just not ready for someone like him. Why don't you go to the whorehouse and work off some of that energy?"

"Well, what are we gonna do, then?" Jack said. "Is he gonna let it go, or try to stop us?"

"I gotta admit, I'm just not sure about that," Ed said. Not hardly."

Chapter Thirteen

Clint knew the youngster, Jack, wanted to try him. It was lucky for the boy that Ed was smarter. But he knew if he stayed in town, it would probably happen. Clint wondered if he would be able to talk Ed out of the bank robbery if Jack wasn't around. Ed was the voice of reason, but it seemed like Jack had hatched the bank robbery idea. At his age, Jack was probably just tired of babysitting cows.

Ed said he was friends with Sheriff Sills. Clint wondered if the lawman had any influence on him. He decided to stop at the sheriff's office next.

He walked to the lawman's office and entered. Sills was sitting with his feet up on his desk.

"Adams," he said, dropping his feet to the floor. "What can I do for you?"

"I had a talk with a man named Ed. He says he's a friend of yours."

"I know a few Eds."

"This one says he intends to rob the bank," Clint said. "He asked me to help him."

"What?"

"He also said you were going to be in on it."

"He's crazy," Sills said. "I ain't robbin' no bank."

"Well then, maybe you can stop them."

"Ah, I don't think Ed's serious," Sills said.

"What about his young friend, Jack?"

Sills sat up in his chair.

"That kid's a hothead."

"Can't Ed control him?"

"Not as much as he used to," Sills said. "Ed could usually keep Jack out of trouble."

"Well, it looks like it might be Jack getting Ed into trouble," Clint said. "Seems robbing the bank was his idea."

"That kid's wild."

"Tell me, Sheriff," Clint said, "what did Ed do before he started working cattle?"

"I knew Ed ten years ago," Sills said. "He rode with some gangs, pulled a few jobs. Then he stopped."

"And when did you see him again?"

"I became sheriff here five years ago," Sills said. "Ed rode in a couple of years back, got a job at the Bar-H. He met Jack there, and they got close."

"Did Ed tell Jack about his past?"

"He might've."

"Sheriff," Clint said, "I don't intend to help them rob the bank."

"Well, I don't either."

"Then maybe we can both stop them."

"I still ain't sure they're serious," Sills said. "Look, there's something else you should know."

"What's that?"

"Ed used to be pretty good with a gun. And Jack thinks he's pretty fast."

"So I assume you won't approach them about the bank."

"I wouldn't wanna push them into anythin'."

"Like going for their guns?" Clint asked. "I wondered about that, too."

"They're not likely to try the Gunsmith," Sills said, "But me? They'd gun me down in a minute."

"Is that what you're afraid of? Is that badge getting a little bit heavy for you?"

Sills looked down at his chest.

"Yeah, maybe it is." He looked at Clint. "I ain't gonna be much help to you, Mr. Adams."

"I think I knew that," Clint said. "I just wanted to find out more about Ed."

"So you're stayin' in town?" Sills asked.

"I am."

"Why?"

"To tell you the truth, I'm not sure I know."

***

Clint thought about going to The Purple Heart to talk to Minerva. But then he thought of some other people he could talk to first. Finch and his bartender cousin, Byron—one of them might know some more about Ed Gregory and Jack Eads. Clint thought the easiest way to rob a bank would be at closing, so if they were going to do it today, he had a few hours. If their plan wasn't in place yet, then maybe he had a day or two. He wanted to get this over with and get out of town. Obviously, his intention to stay out of other people's business was difficult to keep.

He walked to the livery, and found Finch bent over a mare's left leg.

"Oh, hey, Mr. Adams," Finch said. He released the mare's leg and stood up. "What can I do for ya? Your Tobiano is doin' just fine."

"That's good to hear, Finch," Clint said, "but I'm here about something else."

"What's that?"

"Do you know a couple of cowhands named Ed Gregory and Jack Eads?"

"Hmm," the hostler said, thinking, "Gregory sounds familiar. Yeah, he's been in here and time or two."

"What do you know about him?"

"Not much. He works for the Bar-H. Come to think of it, he always has a young fella with him."

"That'd be Eads."

"The impression I got from him was that he thought of himself as some kind of gun slick.

"And Gregory?"

"He don't seem like he's got nothin' to prove," Finch said. "Why you askin'?"

"I'm going to have some trouble with them, and I want to know what I'm up against. You think your cousin might know more?"

"Well," Finch said, "He is a bartender," as if it explained everything,

"Yeah, that's what I was thinking," Clint said. "I'll have a talk with him."

"What kind of trouble you talkin' about?" Finch asked. "If it don't involve guns I'm your man." He held out his hands. "I can use these to back you up."

"I'll keep that in mind, Finch. Thanks."

Clint left the stable and headed for the Black & White Saloon.

Chapter Fourteen

When Clint entered the Black & White it was as lazy and empty as ever. Byron was leaning on the bar, looking bored, and there was one man seated at a table.

"Well," Byron said, "what brings you back here?"

"Beer," Clint said.

Byron set it down and said, "My beer ain't that good. What else brings ya here?"

He asked Byron the same questions he asked Finch.

"Ed Gregory," he said. "Yeah, I know Ed. Showed up in town a couple of years ago. Came here a few times until he discovered some of the other saloons."

"You remember him as the type to look for trouble?" Clint asked.

"Naw, not Ed," Byron said, "but that raw kid that follows him around? He's gonna find the trouble he's lookin' for one of these days."

"That's what I figured."

"You havin' trouble with them?"

"I expect to."

"Guns?"

"Maybe."

"Well, that kid considers himself a gunny, but if you're facin' them I'd take Ed, first. He's more likely to shoot straight."

"Yeah, I got the same impression."

"Are you gonna need somebody to watch your back?" Byron asked. "I've got a shotgun under the bar."

"Leave it there, Byron," Clint said. "I'll handle any trouble myself. I was just looking for something that would give me an edge, like what you said about Ed and Jack."

"Somebody out at the Bar-H might be able to tell you more," Byron suggested.

"You're probably right, but I don't know that I have the time to ride out there."

"You don't have to," Byron said. "That fella over there works on the Bar-H. He might know something."

Clint finished his beer and set the mug down. He tossed a coin onto the bar. "Thanks for the beer, and the information."

"I didn't give you much."

"You gave me enough," Clint said. "Thanks."

He turned and walked to the man seated at the table. He was staring into a half-full beer mug.

"Can I buy you a drink?" Clint asked.

The man looked up at him.

"Why?" the man asked.

"I need to talk to someone who works the Bar-H."

"No problem, then," the man said. "I'll have a whis-key."

"Byron," Clint called out, "whiskey for my friend, and another beer."

Byron came over and put both glasses on the table. The Bat-H hand picked up the whiskey and knocked it back.

"What's your name?" Clint asked.

"Tommy Lang."

"How long have you been at the Bar-H."

"Oh, about ten years."

Lang looked to be over forty.

"Cowhand?"

"Yes, and a good one."

"Do you know Ed Gregory and Jack Eads?"

"Well, yeah, I know 'em."

"What can you tell me about them?"

"I don't like 'em," Tommy said. "Neither one of them is a good cowhand. And that kid, he thinks he's some kind of fast gun."

"Has he ever shot anyone?"

"No, up to now, Ed's kept a reign on him."

"Tell me something," Clint said, "does Ed control Jack, or is it the other way around?"

"You know," Tommy said, "I wonder about that, my-self."

Chapter Fifteen

Clint left The Black & White Saloon and headed for The Purple Heart. He really hadn't learned anything new about Ed and Jack, but what he had thought earlier had been confirmed. Ed was the one he needed to keep his eye on. At some point he would probably let Jack Eads loose.

He entered the busy Purple Heart and went right to the bar. Before he could say a word the bartender said, "You can go right up."

"Thanks."

He made his way through the crush of people to the stairs, and up. When he reached her door he knocked.

"Come in."

He opened the door and entered. Minerva was seated at her dressing table, and looked at him in the mirror.

"I didn't expect to see you again so soon," she said. She stood and turned, and he admired the way her floor length, purple robe clung to the curves of her body.

"I made some progress," he told her.

"Really? Then you'll have to sit and tell me about it."

There were comfortable armchairs in the room, and a sofa against one wall. There was no bed, which told him there must be another room. Clint took an armchair. Minerva took the other chair.

"Tell me what happened?"

"I talked to both men, told them I wouldn't be helping them rob the bank."

"And? Did they try to kill you?"

"Not at all," Clint said. "They accepted everything I said, and said they hoped I wouldn't get in their way."

"And will you?"

"If I can," Clint said. "I also talked to the sheriff."

"I'm sure he was no help, at all."

"You're right, he's afraid."

"He said that?"

"Not in so many words, but I can't count on him for any help."

"Do you think he'll throw in with them?"

"He says he won't, but who knows?"

"So it could be only you against three men?" she asked.

"That's possible."

"Can you find anyone to help you?"

"I haven't been in town long enough to meet anyone," he said.

"What about bringing someone in from out of town?" she asked.

"I don't think I have time," he said. "Besides, I'd have to send telegrams. Is there a key in town?"

"Not yet," she said, "but soon. But I see your point. I guess you only have me."

"I wouldn't expect you to take part in trying to stop a robbery."

"I usually handle my own problems, Mr. Adams."

"Call me Clint."

"And I'm Minerva."

"Not Minnie?"

"Never!" She stood up. "I have some brandy here, Would you like some?"

"Sure."

She walked across the room to a sideboard and poured two glasses. He enjoyed watching her walk away, and back. He accepted the glass.

"Let's sit on the sofa," she said.

"All right."

He stood and walked to the sofa with her. She sat close to him.

"What are you going to do next?" she asked.

"I think I'll check out the bank," he said. "See how susceptible it might be to a robbery."

"You'll do that today?"

"Maybe tomorrow."

"You don't think they'll try to rob the bank today?" she asked.

"I don't think they have a plan, yet. It'll probably be a day or two."

"Couldn't they just rush in and shoot the place up?" she asked.

"They claim they're not looking to kill anyone."

"And you believe them?"

"They're not prepared to have a posse pursue them for bank robbery," Clint said. "I don't think they want to be chased down for murder."

"Well," she said, "I suppose if you're not going to be busy the rest of the day, we could get to know each other a little better."

Before he could reply, she leaned in and kissed him. He leaned into her and returned the kiss.

When she drew back she leaned over to set her glass down, then stood. She undid the belt of her robe and allowed it to fall to the floor. He caught his breath at the sight of her naked body. Her breasts were full and round, topped by dark nipples that had already hardened.

"Think we can do that?" she asked. "Get to know each other better?"

"I think so," he said, coming to his feet.

Chapter Sixteen

Clint took Minerva into his arms and the kiss went on for some time. He ran his hands down her bare back until he could cup her ass cheeks. She writhed against him, mashing her solid breasts against his chest, and then backed away from him.

"Come with me," she said. She took his hand and led him to her bedroom.

In the center of the room was a large, four poster bed. She turned to face him. "We'll need to get those clothes off. And that gun."

Clint started to unbutton his shirt. He said to Minerva, "The gun has to stay close."

"Do you think I'm trying to distract you?"

"The gun always has to remain close."

"I suppose given your reputation, I'll have to understand that. We can hang the gunbelt from the bedpost."

"That'll do," he said. He tossed the shirt aside and unbuckled the gunbelt. He hung it on the bedpost, where he would be able to get to it easily.

Minerva turned down the bed while Clint removed his boots and trousers, while keeping his eyes on her naked form. For a woman over forty, she was in amazing physical condition.

She crawled onto the bed, leaned on her left side and watched while he finished undressing.

"You're in wonderful shape for a man your age," she commented.

"I was about to say the same to you," he said, "about a woman your age."

She laughed, completely unoffended.

Clint climbed on the bed with her, found the mattress extremely firm.

"And now," she said, running her hand down his chest, "to get better acquainted." She moved her hand to his lap and closed it around his swollen penis.

She kissed him, while stroking him to total fullness. He returned the kiss with vigor, and bore her down onto her back. Her mouth opened to accept his tongue and offer her own.

He broke the kiss and moved his mouth along her neck to her upper chest, and then to her breasts. He covered one firm mound with kisses, and then the other. After that he turned his attention to her dark nipples, sucking on them until they were each fully distended. She moaned all through his ministrations, cupping his head in her hands.

He worked his way down her body, kissing her belly, sticking his tongue into her navel. Finally, he nestled comfortably between her long legs, pressing his face to the fragrant forest of hair, there. He poked his tongue through the bush and found her wet and waiting.

"Oh God," she groaned, grabbing his head. "Oh yes . . ."

Clint kept his tongue moving until he pushed her over the edge and a shudder ran through her . . .

***

Later it was her turn. She took her time running her mouth over him, working her way down his body until she was rubbing her cheek over the smooth skin of his hard penis. She ran it all over her face, enjoying the feel and heat of it, and then finally opened her mouth and took it in. She sucked it, slowly at first, allowing it to glide between her lips, and then more avidly, until he let out a guttural roar . . .

***

They laid together, getting their breath back, and then Clint rolled her over and took her from behind. They were both grunting and rutting, the bed jumping beneath them, until they both slumped to the mattress, catching their breath, again.

Minutes later Clint got to his feet and began to dress. Minerva rolled onto her stomach and watched him. When he was strapping on his gun she said, "Leave the money on the dresser."

"What?"

"Did you think I was free?" she asked.'

"You're a whore?"

"In many ways," she said. "Everything I do, I do for money."

"I wish I'd known that before I came up here."

"Why? What difference does it make?"

"I don't pay for sex," he said. "Never have, never will."

"You're kidding."

"I'm not."

Minerva got to her feet and pulled on her robe with her back to him. She turned, tightening her robe.

"I don't give it away for free, Mr. Adams," she told him. "Never have, never will. Just put the money on the dresser."

"Can't do it, Minerva."

"Are you actually serious?" she asked.

"Very."

"If you walk out that door without leaving any money, you can't ever come back."

"And what about the bank?"

"That's something else," she said. "I expect you to keep your word."

"Did I give you my word?" Clint asked and walked out.

Chapter Seventeen

Clint went down to the bar.

"Give me a beer," he told Ken, the bartender.

"Here ya go," Ken said, setting it down in front of him. "Finished upstairs?"

"For good, I think," Clint said.

"Really?" Ken asked, "She's usually pretty good."

"She was fine," he said. "I just wouldn't pay."

Ken stared at him, then laughed.

"Really? I wish I could've seen the look on her face."

"Go on up," Clint said, "it's probably still there."

"Oh no," Ken said. "The time for me to go up is when that look is gone."

Clint drank his beer down.

"Did she tell you about the bank?" Clint asked.

"That somebody plans to rob it? Yeah. You gonna stop it?"

"I said I'd try."

"Got anybody to back you?"

"No, but there's only two of them," Clint answered. "I should be able to handle them."

"I hope you do," Ken said. "I've got a small account there, myself. You want another drink?"

"No, I'm going to my hotel," Clint said. "I want to take a look at that bank in the morning."

"Well, I hope you can keep it from being robbed."

"I think I'm good, as long as they don't intend to rob it overnight."

***

"Whataya mean, we're gonna rob it overnight?" Jack asked. "I thought we was gonna get the Gunsmith blamed."

"That's not gonna work," Ed said.

"Then why rob it tonight?"

"To get it over with," Ed said. "And by the time anybody notices in the mornin', we'll be long gone."

"How are we gonna get in?" Jack asked.

"The bank manager works late, after it closes," Ed said. "He's gonna let us in and open the safe."

"Are we gonna kill 'im?"

"There's no reason to," Ed said. "Our faces are gonna be covered. We just have to be careful not to call each other by name."

"Why would we do that?"

Ed didn't answer.

"Ed?" Jack stared across the table in the Gold Mine Saloon.

"We're not," Ed said was suddenly hit by an idea. "Jack, you've gotta make sure you call me Clint. Get it?"

"Naw, I don't—oh, wait a minute." Jack smiled. "Yeah, I do get it. When do we do this?"

Ed looked at his pocket watch and said, "Any minute now. If the manager sticks to his schedule he should be locking the door any minute." Ed tossed back the remainder of his whiskey. "Come on!"

***

Ed Gregory had pulled after-hours bank jobs, before. The front door was locked, the street in front was empty, the businesses on either side had closed, as expected.

"Now what?" Jack asked, as they approached the bank.

"Now we knock."

"Why don't we have our horses out here?" Jack asked.

"Because we don't want horses to be seen out in front of the closed bank."

"Is he gonna let us in?"

Ed took his gun from his holster and said, "He better."

"If we fire a shot it's gonna bring people runnin'," Jack said.

"He's not gonna think about that when he's lookimn' down the barrel of a gun," Ed assured him.

He used the barrel of his gun to knock on the glass of the door. When there was no answer he knocked again. He could see the door to the bank manager's office open and a portly man appeared at the door. He knocked again, which brought the man across the bank floor.

"We're closed!" he snapped.

"What?" Ed said.

The manager pressed his fleshy cheek to the glass and said again, "We're closed."

Ed pressed the barrel of the gun to the window so that the manager was staring right down the black hole.

"You *were* closed," he said. "You just reopened."

The manager's eyes popped and he swallowed. As he snapped the lock open, Ed breathed a sigh of relief. If the man had given it some thought he would have realized that Ed couldn't shoot. It would have attracted too much attention. And if he killed the manager, who would open the safe. But the manager didn't think, he just reacted. He unlocked the door and stepped back. Ed and Jack stepped inside, both now holding their guns.

"Make sure that door is locked," Ed said to Jack.

"Right," Jack said.

Ed gestured to the manager with his gun and said, "We're here to make a withdrawal."

Chapter Eighteen

Clint woke the next morning, intending to walk to the bank and look it over before going to the cafe for breakfast. But while walking down the street he found himself thinking about Minerva Dawson. Why would a woman like her label herself a whore? What was the point? This question was something that once again tugged at his curiosity.

As he approached the small brick building that housed the bank, he saw the front door was wide open and people were clustered out front. He had a bad feeling that he had waited too long.

As he came closer he saw Sheriff Sills in among the people.

"Sheriff," he called.

Sills separated himself from the small crowd and walked over to Clint.

"You don't wanna be here," he said.

"What's going on?" Clint asked.

"The bank was robbed last night."

"After hours?"

"That's right."

"Does anybody know who robbed it?"

"The bank manager, Mr. Hazleton, mentioned one name."

"And what name was that?"

"He said one of the robbers called the other one 'Clint' twice."

"That's the only name?"

"Yeah."

"Can I talk to the manager?"

"No."

"Why not?"

"They killed him. He was hit on the head, probably with a gun. The doctor says they cracked his skull. He managed to mention your name just before he died."

"Why are you out here, Sheriff?"

"I'm the law," he said. "When the bank teller got to work and found Mr. Hazleton on the floor, he came and got me."

"And who are all these people?"

"Depositors," Sills said. "They're all worried about their money."

"And did you tell them who robbed the bank?" Clint asked.

"How would I know that?" Sills asked.

"The same way I know it," Clint said. "You know Ed and Jack."

"I know them," Sills said. "I don't know that they robbed the bank."

"They said they were going to do the job," Clint reminded him.

"But did they?" Sills asked. "We don't know that."

"Have you decided to take that badge seriously?"

"I'm just doin' my job, Mr. Adams."

"Are you going to track the bank robbers?"

"Well," Sills said, "all I know now is that one of them was named Clint."

"No," Clint said, "you know that one of the robbers called the other 'Clint.' Did they have masks on their faces?"

"Yes."

"How do you know that?"

"Mr. Hazleton said so," Sills said.

"Then the bank manager had more to say than the name 'Clint.' "

"I suppose so."

"What's the doctor's name?"

"Doc Rivers."

"Where's his office?"

"Above the hardware store."

"Is that where the manager's body is?"

Sills shook his head and said, "He's at the undertaker's."

Clint looked over at the small crowd of people who were watching them.

"So this was their plan?" Clint said. "To rob the bank and have it blamed on me. And for you to go along with it."

"Nobody can prove you did it."

"These townspeople don't care if they can prove it," Clint said. "They'll all just come after me."

"And you can gun them down," Sills said. "I can't do anything about it."

Clint looked at the crowd again.

"I'm not going to gun down any of these people," Clint said.

"So what are you gonna do?"

"Go find Ed and Jack and get the money back," Clint said. "How much are we talking about?"

"The teller is figuring that out now," Sills said. "That's what these people are waiting for."

Clint hadn't seen more people arrive, but suddenly the crowd was twice the size, and they all had their angry eyes on him.

"Go back to your people, Sheriff," Clint said. "I'm going to talk to the doctor. After that, I'll track Ed and Jack down and bring them back, with the money. Before I leave, I'll expect you to tell me how much they got."

"Yeah, sure."

Clint turned and walked away, feeling all the eyes on his back.

Chapter Nineteen

Doc Rivers was tall and elderly who looked at Clint over his wire-framed glasses.

"Did he say anything else?" Clint asked.

"No," Rivers said. "Just that they wore masks, and one called the other by name."

"And the name was 'Clint.' "

"Yes," Rivers said. "Your name, right?"

"That's right."

"But you didn't do it."

"Right again."

"Do you know who did?"

"Yes."

"Can you prove it?"

"Not yet."

"So what do you intend to do?" Rivers asked.

"I'm going to track them down," Clint said, "and bring them back, with the money."

"You think you can do that?"

"Yes."

"Why wouldn't you just mount up, ride out and never look back?" the doctor asked. "Before the townspeople can come after you."

"I can't do that, Doctor," Clint said. "I can't have that black mark on my name."

"You mean the name The Gunsmith?"

"That's right," Clint said. "I'm not a bank robber."

"Then you'd better leave town today," the doctor said, "and return with the money."

"My intention is to return with the robbers *and* the money."

"The money would satisfy the town."

"They killed the manager," Clint said. "I want them to pay for that."

"You can make them pay by leaving them out there when you find them."

"You mean kill them?" Clint shook his head. "Not if I don't have to."

Rivers studied Clint for a few moments, then asked, "Why do I get the feeling you don't exactly live up to your reputation as a killer?"

"I'm not a bank robber, and I'm not a killer," Clint said. "I'm a man who won't stand still for being labeled either."

"I understand."

"You know your sheriff isn't going to do anything."

"Of course not. He's not a real lawman."

"If the townspeople would be willing to do something about me, why not do something about him?"

"I'm on the Town Council," the doctor said. "If you get back—"

"*When* I get back," Clint corrected.

"—when you get back, I'll take it up with the Council."

"Thanks for your time, Doctor."

"Good luck, Mr. Adams."

"Thanks."

Rather than give the townspeople more time to come after him, Clint decided to bypass a trip to the undertaker. He went directly to the livery stable.

As he entered Finch came walking over, leading the saddled Tobiano.

"I heard what happened," he said. "Thought you'd want to get out of town fast."

"You don't believe I robbed the bank?"

"Not a chance."

"Did those two fellas, Ed and Jack, have their horses here?"

"No," Finch said, "I don't know where they kept 'em. But I know Gregory rides a Morgan with one cleft hoof."

"Which one?"

"Front left. It's got a bar horseshoe on it."

"How do you know?"

"I put it there last month."

"Okay, thanks, Finch." Clint took the reins and mounted up. "I'm not going back to the hotel for my gear."

"No problem." Finch walked to the back of the stable, returned with saddlebags and a Winchester.

"Not much in the bags, but there's some coffee, a pot, and beef jerky."

"You're a good man, Finch."

"I can get your gear from the room and hold it here until you come back."

"You believe I'm coming back?" Clint asked.

"With those two bank robbers, and the money," Finch said. "In fact, I'll saddle up and go with you, if you want."

"No," Clint said, "stay here. I don't know how long this'll take." He started toward the door, then turned his horse around. "See you when I get back, Finch. I'll buy you a beer."

"I'll hold you to that."

Finch followed Clint out.

"If you ride down Main Street past the bank people are liable to try and grab you. I'd go out the other end of town and then circle around."

"Good advice," Clint said. "But I need to find the tracks they left, to see which way they rode."

"You'll be takin' a big chance with the crowd on Main Street. You might have to kill some of them."

"I don't want to do that," Clint said. "All right, I'll ride out the north end, check the ground for that bar shoe track. If I don't see it I'll take that south road into town. Hopefully, they stayed on the road, figuring nobody would be following them."

"Good luck, Clint."

"I'll see you soon."

Clint turned his horse and rode north.

Chapter Twenty

Clint rode out of town to the north, started circling, looking at the ground. There were plenty of tracks, but none with a bar shoe. He was going to have to circle around to the south end. He could have ridden through town, but Finch was right. He would have had to kill someone to make his point. This was costing him time, but it was worth it.

He didn't know how much of a head start Ed and Jack had on him, but they had been travelling at night. They couldn't have gone very fast, or far.

Riding around Kennelworth to the south side took the better part of an hour. He was careful not to be seen. When he got there he started studying the road out of town. As with the north there were plenty of tracks, but this time that bar shoe stood out. Once he had it spotted, he started to follow it.

They were continuing south, and if they kept going that way, they were headed for Nevada. Clint wondered if they were simply going to drift, or if they had a destination in mind. He wondered if they even knew, since the bank robbery seemed to have been rushed. He assumed the two men figured they'd better get it done before he took steps to stop them. He felt responsible for the robbery, and the death of the manager, since he had already known they were going to rob it. He should have acted more quickly, rather than letting the night go by, assuming the bank would be safe after hours. He had wasted too much time with Minerva Dawson, and felt foolish for more reasons than one. Now he either had to catch them and bring them back, with the money, or be branded a bank robber. He wished he knew how much money they had absconded with, but it made more sense to get as early a start as possible, and avoid an encounter with an angry mob. Since the bank was the only one in town, he assumed there would have been at least twenty thousand on deposit, much of it belonging to Minerva Dawson, the lady whore and businesswoman.

Clint followed the tracks until almost dark, when he camped for the night. Thanks to the hostler, he supped on coffee and beef jerky, and slept near a warm fire. In the morning he had some more coffee and bacon—a hunk of which was a nice surprise from Finch—then killed the fire and got back on the trail.

By this time there was enough familiar about both horse's tracks that he could have followed either one. In the event the two men split up, however, he would have kept on the trail of the horse with the bar shoe. He hoped they wouldn't separate, as then it would take him twice as long to track them both.

The second day he could see from the tracks that he was getting closer. He stopped at their last campfire, dismounted, found there were still some warm ashes. He also found a couple of empty cans of beans. He thought they would want to stop for supplies, if all they were eating was beans. He figured he should catch up to them sometime the next day.

He mounted up, figuring to ride a couple of more hours.

***

Some miles ahead, Ed Gregory reined his horse in, turned in his saddle to look behind him.

"You expectin' a posse?" Jack Eads asked.

"Naw," Ed said, "I don't figure on that."

"What are ya lookin' for, then?"

"I don't know," Ed said, "I just got a feelin'."

Jack stared off into the distance.

"I don't see nothin'."

"Neither do I," Ed said, "but I got a feelin'."

"'bout what?"

"Adams."

"You think the Gunsmith's gonna come after us?" Jack asked. "They probably strung him up by now."

"Maybe."

"Well then," Jack said, "we better keep movin' don't ya think?"

Ed stopped looking behind them and looked at Jack.

"There's a small town just ahead." He said, "Siringo. We'll stop there for supplies."

"Good," Jack said. "I'm tired of beans."

***

As they rode into Siringo Jack said, "Ed, we ain't even counted the money yet."

Ed touched the saddlebags the bank money was in.

"There's time for that."

"Yeah, but when are we gonna split it?"

"There's time for that, Jack," Ed said. "Let's just make damn sure it's ours."

"You still thinkin' about Adams?"

"Adams, or anybody else," Ed said. "Let's outfit here to make sure we can make Nevada. We can split the money there, and you can go your own way, if you want."

"I never said nothin' about that, Ed," Jack said. "I'd just like to hold my own share of the money in my own greedy little hands."

"Don't worry," Ed said, as they stopped in front of the town's mercantile store, "you will."

Chapter Twenty-One

When Clint came to Siringo he stopped in front of the mercantile. It was a small town and there weren't a lot of tracks in the street. The bar-shoe stood out. He dismounted and went inside.

There was a bored looking, middle-aged man behind a counter.

"Well now," he said, suddenly brightening, "another customer today."

"You had some others?" Clint asked.

"Two, as a matter of fact. Came in together."

"One young and one older?"

"That's right. Friends of yours?"

"Not friends, but I'm looking for them."

"I thought they seemed shifty. Bought a few supplies and lit out lickety split."

"I guess I'll have to do the same, then," Clint said. "I'll take some coffee, beef jerky and a hunk of bacon. And a couple of cans of peaches. Put it all in a sack."

"Yes, Sir."

Clint waited while the clerk put his supplies in a gunny sack. When the man was done, Clint paid his bill.

"The two men who were here," he said. "How long ago?"

"A few hours, at least."

"Did they talk?"

"They asked me for supplies."

"Did they talk to each other?" Clint asked. "Say anything about where they're heading."

"Naw, they was careful not to say nothin' like that. What'd they do? Why are you huntin' them?"

"They robbed a bank and killed the manager."

"My God!"

"Did they say anything at all to indicate where they were going?"

"No, Sir."

"Okay." Clint picked up his sack of supplies and went out to his horse. He was tying the bag to his saddle when the clerk came out.

"Hey, Mister!"

"Yeah?"

"I came out and watched them ride away," the man said, "like I am you."

"And?"

"They rode out of town and went south."

The bar-shoe tracks told Clint that much, but he said, "Thanks."

"I hope you catch them."

Clint mounted his horse, waved and rode away. South.

***

According to the store clerk, he was about three hours behind them. Apparently, they seemed to have increased their speed. He wasn't closing on them. That meant he was going to have to increase his speed, which meant pushing the Tobiano.

He stopped early that day, meaning to give the Tobiano some time to rest before he pushed him, starting the next morning.

He made himself a meal of bacon-and-beans, washed it down with coffee, then opened a can of peaches for dessert. There was enough grazing for the Tobiano to satisfy himself, and a nearby water hole for them to drink from, and for Clint to refill his canteen.

***

The next morning he made do with a pot of coffee and some cold beef jerky. He doused the fire, saddled up and started south, pushing the Tobiano into a steady trot.

***

"Where are we goin', Ed?" Jack asked. "We ain't headin' south, no more."

"I don't wanna go to Nevada," Ed said. "I prefer Colorado."

"I ain't never been to Colorado," Jack said. "Are we goin' to Denver?"

"No," Ed said.

"Why not?"

"Too big," Ed said.

"Then where?"

Ed didn't look at Jack, but stared straight ahead.

"I'll know it when I see it."

***

Shortly, they crossed the border into Colorado.

"Have you been here before?" Jack asked.

"Yes," Ed said, "years ago. I'm thinking Fort Collins is a likely place."

"They got a big bank?"

"I assume they do."

"We gonna hit it?" Jack asked.

"No," Ed said, "we're gonna use it."

"Use it? For what?"

Ed turned his head and looked at Jack.

"We're gonna make a deposit."

Chapter Twenty-Two

The tracks shifted to the west, and Clint figured they were heading for Colorado. If they made it to Denver, they would be hard to find. Clint would have to ask his private detective friend, Talbot Roper, for his help. But there were several places before that where they might stop.

If they had continued south he probably would have caught up to them by now. Instead he found another campfire with warm ashes, and a bar-shoe imprint in the ground.

"Okay, Toby," he said, stroking the Tobiano's neck, "we're heading west."

***

As they rode into Fort Collins Jack said to Ed, "First thing I'm gonna do is get me a girl."

"You get as many girls as you want."

"I'll need some money."

"We'll talk about that when we get hotel rooms," Ed told him.

"Hey, Ed—"

"There," Ed said, pointing, "that hotel looks good."

Jack looked over at the High Mountain Hotel and said, "Finally. I just wanna get into a room, count that money, get my share and find me a girl."

"We gotta get these horses took care of," Ed said. "There'll be plenty of time to count the money."

"Don't know why we ain't counted it yet," Jack complained.

"You're a hothead, Jack," Ed said. "I just wanted to make sure you didn't do somethin' stupid."

"Why do you think I'm so dumb?" Jack demanded.

"That's easy," Ed said. "You're young. Bein' stupid's your job."

***

By the time Clint rode into Fort Collins there were too many tracks to pick out that bar-shoe. But he had followed the track to just outside town, so he was fairly certain this would be the place Ed and Jack would settle in for a spell.

He found a room at the Hamer House Hotel, a small, one story place. He never liked ground floor rooms in hotels, but he didn't want to waste time looking for another place, when he could spend it looking for Ed and Jack.

He obtained a room that was away from the front of the hotel, then tucked the Tobiano away in a livery stable down the street.

He asked the hostler if anyone had ridden into town on a Morgan with one bar-shoe. Any hostler worth his salt would notice that sort of thing.

"No bar-shoes here, Mister," the old man said. "I don't like 'em and if I see a horse sportin' one, I'd do what I could to fix it."

"Okay, thanks. Are there many liveries in town?"

"There's three more, on First Street, Fifth Street, and Powell Street."

"Okay, thanks."

Clint left the livery with his rifle and saddlebags and walked to the hotel. Normally, when tracking somebody, he would have stopped at the local sheriff's office or Police station, but while he was under suspicion of robbing a bank himself, he chose not to announce his presence.

If Ed and Jack were indeed in Fort Collins, it had taken longer to track them down than he expected. The town was growing by leaps and bounds, with stone quarrying, sugar-beet farming, and the slaughter of sheep among the area's earliest industries. The sheer size of the town was going to make it a challenge to find Ed and

Jack. Clint decided it would be easier to find Ed's Morgan, with the bar-shoe.

After leaving his gear in his room he went looking for a hot meal. He found several eateries within walking distance of the hotel, and chose one. He decided to have a steak while he could. Who knew when he would be able to have another?

The time of day was between lunch and supper, so there were more empty tables then occupied ones. He had plenty of leg room, and took his time consuming the meat and vegetables that overflowed from his plate, washing it down with mugs of ice cold beer. He didn't think he had found the best restaurant in town, but it would do.

After his meal he made a point of marking his location, and figuring out where to go first, Powell, First or Fifth Street. It turned out he was walking distance from First Street.

The First Street livery was small, and didn't have a horse with a bar-shoe in residence. The hostler there had never seen one.

He walked to Fifth Street to the No. 5 Livery Stable—an odd name since there were only four in town. It turned out he would have no need of checking the livery on Powell Street.

"Bar-shoe, front left. Yeah, fella brought that one in yesterday."

"Is it still here?"

"Sure is," the middle-aged man said. "I tried to get him to let me replace it, but he said he didn't care."

"Can I see it?"

"Right over here."

Clint followed the hostler deeper into the stable til they came to a stall with a big Morgan in it. Clint checked the front left foot and found what he was looking for.

"That it?" the man asked.

"That's it." Clint stepped out of the stall and rubbed his hands together. "Did he have another man with him?"

"Yeah, a young one. He didn't look happy."

"How do you mean?"

"He was impatient about somethin'."

"Did they give you any idea where they were staying?" Clint asked.

"Not really, but the nearest hotel to here is the High Mountain Hotel, a couple of streets down," the hostler said, pointing.

"Thanks."

The man walked him outside and said, "I'd be careful if I was you. They weren't a nice pair."

"Thanks," Clint said. "I'll keep that in mind."

He started to walk away. When he reached the hotel he approached the desk clerk.

"Two men checked in yesterday," he said, taking a dollar from his pocket. "What rooms are they in?"

The clerk took the dollar and gave Clint two room numbers.

Chapter Twenty-Three

They were in rooms fourteen and sixteen. Clint figured they were using the bank money to get separate rooms. He listened intently at both doors and heard nothing. If neither one was in their room, then where was the money?

He went back downstairs. Two more dollars got him a master key. He didn't want either man to come back and find their door damaged. He opened fourteen first, searched it and found nothing but a rifle and some saddlebags. He looked in the saddlebags, didn't even find an extra shirt. Next, he went to room sixteen. It was neater, and felt like an older man's room. He was convinced it was Ed's room. It might have been neater, but still there was no sign of the bank money in either one. That could only mean one thing—Ed was carrying the money with him.

***

"I don't understand him," Jack said to his whore. She was naked, lying next to him, long and lean with smooth skin and hardly any breasts. She was about five years older than Jack, but neither of them minded. Her name was Lola.

"Don't understand what, lover?" she asked, stroking his hard cock.

"Why rob a bank, then take the money and put it in another bank? It doesn't make sense to me."

"It does to me," she told him.

"Really? Explain it, then."

"It's simple," she said. "Nobody would expect it."

"I suppose not," Jack said. "I just wish I had my share."

"When do you think you'll get it?" she asked, eager to get her hands on it.

"I don't know," he said, "but it better be soon."

She reached down and cupped his balls in one hand, while stroking him with the other.

"Ain't you better than him with a gun?" she asked. "Ain't that what you said?"

He stretched out on the bed while she used her hands on him.

"If I was you," she said, "I'd take that money from him. How much is it?"

"I don't even know," Jack said. "He ain't told me."

She kissed his neck and began working her way down his body with her mouth. When she reached his crotch she looked up at him, saw him looking down at her.

"I'm gonna do this for you, Jack," she said, flicking her tongue out and licking the head of his penis, "and then we'll figure out how to get that money from him."

Before he could say a word, she swooped down and took the entire length of his penis into her mouth . . .

***

Lola came downstairs and went to Madame Janelle's office. The portly, middle-aged madame was seated behind her desk.

"Well?" she said.

"He's a big talker," Lola said. "Claims him and his partner robbed a bank in Utah."

"How much?"

"He says he don't know, only his partner knows."

"Can you find out, sweetie?"

"Oh, yes," Lola said. "I'll find out. He says his partner put the money in a bank here in Fort Collins."

"Why the hell would he do that?" Janelle asked.

"I'm thinkin' he don't think nobody would look for it there."

"He's probably right about that."

"He claims to be good with a gun," Lola said, "so I'm gonna get him to use it on his partner, and get that money."

"You do that, Lola," Janelle said, "you get that money for us."

Lola smiled, nodded and headed back upstairs.

Chapter Twenty-Four

When Clint found nothing in the two hotel rooms he went down to the front desk.

"Can I see the register again?" he asked waving another dollar beneath the young man's nose.

"Sure." He turned the book around.

Clint looked at the two names of the men who had checked in the day before. The names were 'Jack Smith' and 'Ed Jones.'" The fact that the first names were the same as the men Clint was looking for confirmed their identity for him.

"You got any idea where they are?" he asked.

"No, Sir."

"Any idea where they took their meals yesterday, or today?"

"No, Sir."

Clint was thinking he might have to keep watch on the hotel and wait for them to return, but then he thought of something. Jack Eads was a young man who had just spent time on the trail.

"Tell me something," Clint said. "Where's the nearest whorehouse?"

***

The clerk directed Clint to Madame Janelle's, which was several blocks from the hotel. It was a plain looking, two-story wooden structure which did not look like a whorehouse.

He decided not to wait outside, as Jack or Ed might not even be inside. No, instead he walked up to the front door and knocked. A stately, tall red-head answered the door. When she didn't see a badge on Clint's chest she stopped holding her robe closed. It opened to reveal an impressive set of breasts, with freckles between them.

"Can I help you, handsome?" she asked.

"I'd like to see Madame Janelle."

"Really?" she asked. "My name's Ophelia. Are you sure I won't do?"

"On any other day you'd do fine," Clint said. "Today I need to see the boss."

The girl frowned and plucked at her robe, ready to close it again.

"Are you law?"

"I'm not, and I'm not a bounty hunter, but I am looking for a couple of outlaws."

"And you think they're here?"

"They just arrived in town yesterday, after many days on the trail. What do you think?"

"After a hot meal I guess they'd come here," Ophelia said. "Wait a minute and I'll tell Madame Janelle you're here. Do you have a name?"

"Clint Adams," he said, deciding to tell the truth.

"Oh my," Ophelia said. "Just wait right here, Mr. Adams."

She backed up and closed the door. Moments later she reappeared, her robe tightly cinched.

"Madam Janelle will see you now."

As Clint had told Minerva, he had never paid for a whore. He had, however, known many whores and Madams and had found most of them decent people.

Ophelia led him down a long hall to a door that was ajar, and showed him into the presence of sixtyish Madam, seated behind a desk.

"Is this on the level?" the woman asked him. "You're the Gunsmith?"

"That's right."

"That'll be all, Ophelia."

The redhead looked unhappy about being dismissed, left the room and closed the door.

"Ophelia said you're looking for two men," Janelle said.

"Two outlaws," Clint said. "They robbed a bank and killed the manager. I tracked them to Fort Collins."

"What makes you think they're here? In my place?"

"One of them is a young man, in his twenties. After days on the trail where do you think he'd go?"

"After a hot meal? Here."

"He's a hothead and a big mouth. I'm sure he's talked about the robbery."

"He has," Janelle said, deciding to be honest. After all, this was The Gunsmith. She wouldn't have liked to be caught lying to him. "Right now, upstairs with one of my best girls. I don't want her caught in a crossfire."

"She won't be," Clint assured her.

"He's in room eight, with a blonde named Lola.

"May I go up?" he asked.

"You may. It's just you, though, right? No law?"

"No law," he said. "This is personal."

"Just don't shoot up my place."

"I won't." He started for the door, then turned back.

"Do you know if he's said anything about where the money is?" he asked.

She laughed and said to him, "You ain't gonna believe this."

Chapter Twenty-Five

He didn't believe it, yet thought it was a brilliant move. Who would suspect bank robbers would put their booty into another bank?

Clint went up the stairs to the second level and found his way down the hall to room eight. He pressed his ear to the door and heard what he hoped he would. The two people in the room sounded busy.

He turned the doorknob as quietly as he could and inched the door open. A long-limbed blonde with her back to the door was riding a man up and down. He couldn't see the man's face yet, so he didn't know if it was Jack or Ed or somebody else. But Janelle had indicated that it was a young man who talked about robbing a bank.

When he saw the gunbelt and gun sitting on a chair near the action, he recognized the weapon, and now knew the man was Jack.

He decided not to wait until the people had finished. Breaking in on the action would put the man even more off balance. He didn't want the hothead young Jack Eads to go for his gun.

Clint slipped into the room quietly, though he needn't have been that quiet. They were both grunting and groaning loudly. He was able to sidle right up to the bed and press the barrel of his gun to Jack's sweaty face, shocking both of them.

The girl screamed and Jack's eyes bugged out as they both froze.

"What the hell—" Jack snapped.

"Remember me, Jack?"

Jack stared at Clint and then said, "Adams?"

"You can go, Miss," Clint said. "Madam Janelle is waiting downstairs."

She wasted no time climbing off the man and the bed, grabbing her robe, and running from the room.

Jack sat up in the bed and looked over at his gun.

"Go ahead," Clint said, "try it."

"This is the same as shootin' me in the back! Jack complained. "Let me have my gunbelt and we'll do it fair."

"You just stay on that bed. We've got things to talk about."

Clint looked around, saw a chair and pulled it close to the bed, but still out of Jack's reach.

"Can't I get dressed?" Jack asked.

"Pull the sheet up."

Jack grabbed the sheet and pulled it up over his nude body.

"Where's Ed?" Clint asked.

"How the hell do I know?" Jack demanded. "He don't check with me before he does things."

"You mean like putting the bank job money into a bank here in town."

"Yeah, like that," Jack said, with distaste. "That don't make no sense to me."

"Did he bank it all, or just his share?"

"All of it," Jack said. "I still don't even know how much we got."

"And you probably never will," Clint said.

"Whataya mean?" Jack asked, frowning.

"Ed probably plans to kill you and keep the money for himself."

"What makes you say that?"

"Why else do you think you don't have your share, yet?" Clint asked. "You aren't getting your share."

Jack thought about it for a moment, then said, "That sonofabitch."

"Don't worry about it," Clint said. "Neither one of you is going to get to spend it."

"Are you gonna kill us?" Jack asked.

"I should, since the two of you tried to have me blamed for the bank robbery, and for killing the manager."

"So he died?"

"He did. Which one of you hit him?"

Jack turned his eyes away from Clint.

"I hit 'im, but I didn't intend to kill him."

"Well, you did. And you tried to have me blamed."

"That was Ed's idea."

The hotheaded young man Clint had met in Utah had been reduced, in his nudity, to an embarrassed young man. But it wasn't enough for Clint to let him get dressed. Not yet, anyway.

"Are you still willing to put your gun against mine, Jack?" Clint asked.

"Not when I'm naked."

"Well, you won't get the chance, dressed or naked."

Clint walked to the chair and picked up the young man's gunbelt. He tossed it over his shoulder and turned to look at Jack.

"All right," he said, "get dressed and we'll go and find your partner."

Jack tossed the sheet back, stood up and started to get dressed.

"You won't get the drop on Ed the way you did on me," he said.

"You better hope I do, or he'll kill both of us."

Chapter Twenty-Six

When Jack was dressed Clint marched him down the stairs. Madam Janelle was waiting for them at the door.

"How much does he owe you, Madam?" Clint asked.

"Five dollars."

"What? I—"

Clint poked him in the back with his gun.

"Pay the lady."

"It's all I got!" Jack complained.

"Then you should've gotten your cut from Ed," Clint said. "Now neither one of you will get any of it."

Jack handed Janelle five dollars and asked Clint, "What're you gonna do, rob the bank?"

"I'm sure the local bank will return the money when I explain how it came to be deposited with them. Let's go, out the door."

As he pushed Jack past Madam Janelle he said, "Thank you very much."

"You're quite welcome," she said. "Be sure you come back and see us before you leave town."

"Thank you for the invitation."

He followed Jack out.

The outlaw turned to face him.

"Now where to?"

That was a good question.

"Do you know what bank Ed put the money in?" Clint asked.

"No, Ed didn't say."

"What was he going to do today, while you were at the whorehouse."

"He didn't say. He just told me to relax."

"How do you know he's even still in town?" Clint asked. "Maybe he withdrew the money and left."

"If he did that," the younger man said, "I'll track him down and kill him myself."

Now that he was dressed Jack seemed to have regained some of his bravado. Clint decided to cut him down to size.

"Don't worry," he said, "I can take care of both of you."

"So you're gonna kill us," Jack said. "Why didn't you just shoot me while I was in bed?"

"I want that bank money first," Clint said. "After I have that, we'll see."

"So where are we goin' now?" Jack asked.

"Back to your hotel," Clint said. "We'll just wait there for your friend."

"Some friend, if you're right about him leavin' town with the money."

"When we get to your hotel, we'll find out how many banks are in town. After that we'll check them all."

"I don't like walkin' around without my gun."

"Get used to it," Clint said.

***

When they reached the hotel they stopped at the front desk.

"How many banks are there in town?" Clint asked.

"Three, sir." He named them and told Clint where they were located.

"Obliged," Clint said, and they left.

The nearest bank was the First Colorado Bank, a few blocks walking distance.

"We rode past that one on the way into town," Jack said. "That's when Ed got the idea."

"And it's the nearest one to your hotel," Clint said. "I wouldn't think Ed would want to be very far away from that money."

When they reached the one-story, cement building Clint stopped just outside.

"What's wrong?" Jack asked.

"I've got to figure out an approach," Clint said. "They're not going to just tell me how much Ed deposited. They probably won't even say if he opened an account."

"So whatta we gonna do?" Jack asked.

"I can't go to the law," Clint said. "Word has probably gone out that the Gunsmith robbed the bank in Kennelworth, Utah."

"That was Ed's idea," Jack said.

"Yeah, I got that," Clint said. "Well, let's see what they say. The law would know about the Utah bank robbery, but maybe this bank manager won't have heard,"

Clint pushed Jack ahead of him, together they entered the bank. There were three teller's cages. Clint approached the one with a young woman behind it.

"Can I help you, Sir?" she asked with a pretty smile.

"Yes, I'd like to see the bank manager," Clint said.

"That would be Mr. Seagrave," she said. "Can I tell him what it's about?"

Clint suddenly got an idea and said, "Yes, I believe someone is planning to rob your bank."

"Oh, my," she said. "Please wait here."

She left the cage and went to a door with BANK MANAGER written on it. She knocked and entered, reappeared just moments later with a tall man in a three-piece suit right behind her. They both appeared to be very worried. Clint hoped this would work.

Chapter Twenty-Seven

"I'm Mr. Seagrave," the man said to Clint, careful to remain behind the teller's cage.

"Why don't we talk about it in your office, sir?" Clint asked. "I don't want to alarm anyone."

The middle-aged man hesitated. Clint wondered if he was always this pale?

"Yes, very well," Seagrave said. Then he looked at the girl. "Not a word, Susie."

"I understand, Sir."

"Please, follow me," the manager said.

As they came around the cages to follow the man to his office Clint said to Jack, "You open your mouth and I'll put a bullet in it. Got that?"

"I got it."

They entered the man's office and as he went behind his desk Clint closed the door.

"Now, w-what's this about a robbery?" Seagrave asked.

"There's no need to be alarmed right now," Clint said. "There's a man in town who has a reputation for robbing banks. But before he does that, he makes a large deposit. I want to check and see if anyone made such a deposit yesterday or today."

"I can tell you that without checking," Seagrave said. "I had to approve a large deposit just yesterday after-noon."

"How much was it?" Clint asked.

"It was over thirty thousand dollars," Seagrave said. "I have to say, the man didn't look like a fellow who would have that much money."

"That's because he stole that money from the bank in Utah," Clint said. "I've been tracking him, and he led me here. I don't know where he is, but I knew he'd deposit the money here in a local bank."

"Why would he do such a thing?"

"Because he knows no one would expect him to do that."

"Indeed, it makes no sense."

"Except that he's the nervous type. He doesn't want to carry that much around with him, or leave it in his hotel room."

"But he would rob our bank, taking back his own money, plus our depositor's money?"

"It's possible. Or he may stay in town a few days, and then just close his account and withdraw his money."

"So what do you intend to do?"

"I'm going to look for him. But if I don't locate him right away, I'll stay across the street and wait."

"Shouldn't we alert the sheriff?" Seagrave asked.

"We could, but I don't think it's necessary," Clint said. "Besides, the sheriff would just say he can't do anything because the man hasn't broken the law."

"I suppose that's true, but . . . aren't you a lawman?"

"No," Clint said, "the local lawman from Utah wouldn't cross any borders, so I've taken it upon myself to track him down."

"May I ask your name?" Seagrave said.

"Of course," Clint said. "My name is Clint Adams."

Seagrave sat back and stared for a moment, then said. "The Gunsmith?"

"That's right."

Suddenly, Seagrave looked like he was relaxing.

"I have never heard anything about The Gunsmith robbing a bank," he said. "I feel better now. So, you'll keep this man from robbing my bank?"

"I will. But if you'll trust me, I'd like to know exactly how much he deposited."

"Of course." Seagrave stood up. "Wait here." He walked out.

"I know what you're thinkin'," Jack said, speaking for the first time.

"You do?"

"Yep." Jack nodded. "You're gonna get this manager to give you the money."

"Now that's not a bad idea."

"You know, you and me, we could split it and leave Ed out."

"You'd do that to your partner?" Clint asked.

"Why not?" Jack asked. "The more I think about it, the more I'm convinced Ed was gonna do it to me. After hittin' that bank which was my idea."

"Let's see what happens," Clint said.

The manager returned, carrying some papers. He sat down behind his desk.

"Let's see . . . he deposited thirty-one thousand and some change."

"Let's say thirty-one thousand," Clint replied.

"Very well," He put the file down on the desk. "Thirty-one. What would you like me to do?"

"You've got money in your bank that was taken from another bank," Clint said. "I'm sure you want them to get it back."

"Are you going to ask me to give you the money?" Seagrave asked.

"I was thinking about it."

Seagrave hesitated then said, "I would want to send a telegram to the bank."

"No problems. It's the Bank of Kennelworth, Utah Territory."

"I'll send a telegram today," Seagrave said. "If they okay it I'll give you the money."

"As long as you understand it was a small bank. This robbery might have put it out of business. At least, until I bring the money back to them."

"I understand," the bank manager said. "I'll decide one way or another by this afternoon."

"Good. It's better not to leave it overnight. The Kennelworth bank was hit after hours."

"We have after hours security," Seagrave said, "but I understand. I don't want another bank's ill-gotten gains in my bank."

"Okay," Clint said. "I'll come back at closing."

"Very well."

Clint and Jack stood up and started for the door. Clint opened it, then turned back.

"If you have the law waiting for us, I'd understand."

"I won't do that, I assure you. I think I can trust a man with your reputation."

"I'll see you later, then."

Outside the bank Jack asked, "Why'd you say that?"

"What?"

"About not blaming him if he had the law here when we come back."

"Because now he knows I don't care if he does it," Clint said. "And he won't."

"What about the telegram to Kennelworth?"

"That town is a mess," Clint said. "It has no law to speak of, and the bank manager is dead, I doubt they've replaced him by now. Seagrave isn't going to get a reply to his telegram."

"And he'll give you the money," Jack said. "Smart. And then we split thirty-one thousand dollars."

"Not a chance, Jack," Clint said. "In fact, you won't even be there."

"What?" Jack said. "Are you gonna kill me?"

"That'll depend on what happens when we find Ed."

"And if we don't?"

"We will," Clint said. "He'll come back to this bank for his money."

"*His* money?"

"That's the way he'll think of it."

"And what if he comes back before they close to take the money out?"

"That'll be too soon," Clint said. "Come on. We'll wait at your hotel."

"You gonna leave my body there?"

"For now, I'll leave you tied up in your room."

Jack felt better. If Clint Adams didn't kill him, he might decide to split the money. After all, thirty-one thousand was a lot of cash.

Chapter Twenty-Eight

Clint decided to tie Jack up as soon as they got to the room. He put him in an armchair, rather than the flimsier straight-backed wooden chair and trussed him up good.

"You gonna leave me here all day with nothin' to eat or drink?" Jack demanded.

"You bet," Clint said. "I'm thinking you should've spent your last five dollars on food and drink rather than a whore."

"Yeah but—" Jack was saying when Clint gagged him.

"Now I'm going to find a good place to watch for your buddy, Ed," Clint said, patting Jack on the top of his head.

He left the room and went down to the lobby.

"Any sign of Mr. Smith, yet?" he asked the clerk.

"No, Sir."

"Okay, thanks."

"Where will you be, Sir, if he comes in?" the young clerk asked.

"Don't worry," Clint said, "if he comes in anytime from now, I'll see him."

Clint went out the front door, scanned the storefronts across the street for a likely place to put himself.

***

Meanwhile, Ed Gregory had spent the afternoon looking for a place to have a good meal with some good whiskey. When he deposited the Kennelworth bank money in the Fort Collins bank, he had kept a few hundred out for himself. He intended to leave the money in the local bank until he figured out a way of disposing of Jack.

He had the biggest steak he had ever seen, covered with onions and potatoes, and washed it down with half a bottle of good whiskey, rather than the rot gut he usually drank.

"Anythin' else, Sir?" the waiter asked.

"No," Ed said, taking his money out and counting off enough to pay the check. The waiter's eyes widened when he saw the bills in Ed's hands.

When Ed went to the door, staggering a bit, the waiter followed him, then gave a signal to his two confederates across the street. The waiter liked his job, but it didn't pay much, so in occasion—like today—he pointed out a customer to his partners.

As Ed started off down the street, two men stepped from a doorway and followed . . .

Chapter Twenty-Nine

Clint had been in his chosen hidey-hole a good three hours when he saw two uniformed policemen enter the hotel. Apparently, Fort Collins had a modern police department. He had a bad feeling, like maybe the bank manager, Seagrave, had sent for the police. But how would he have known what hotel to send them to?

He waited, tapping his foot impatiently, until the two policemen left, after being inside for roughly twenty minutes. The bad part was that they had Jack with them, his hands free of handcuffs. Depending on what Jack had told them, he could have ruined everything.

Clint felt he had to get that money out of the bank, but first he wanted to know what those policemen wanted, and why they took Jack with them.

He trotted across the street, into the lobby and up to the front desk.

"Oh, Sir—" the clerk started.

"What was that all about?" Clint asked.

"Those policemen told me that Mr. Smith has been killed."

"What? How?"

"Apparently he was robbed. They said his pockets had been turned out, and he must've put up a fight. He was beaten to death."

"And why'd they take the other man?"

"Well, I, uh, told them that he had checked in with Mr. Smith, so they went upstairs and got him. They are taking him to identify the body."

"Ah, Jesus," Clint said, annoyed. It didn't look as if he would be bringing the two bank robbers back to Kennelworth, so he had to make sure he got the money.

"Thanks," he said, and left the hotel, rushing to get to the bank before Jack could tell the police anything.

***

There was still a couple of hours before closing when he reached the bank. As he entered, the teller saw him, turned and hurried to the manager's office. When she came out she rushed to Clint and said, "Please come with me."

He followed her to Seagrave's office.

"You can go in," she said, and walked away.

Clint entered and closed the door behind him. As he approached the desk the manager was tightening the strap on a bank bag.

"Any word on your bank robber?" Seagrave asked.

"Yes," Clint said, "he's dead."

Seagrave stopped what he was doing.

"What?"

"Apparently he kept some money out when he made the deposit, and he was robbed and killed for it.

Seagrave sat down.

"So there's no danger?"

"Apparently not," Clint said, not bothering to point out the fact that Jack was also a bank robber. "Have you had a reply to your telegram?"

"Nothing," Seagrave said. He put his hand on the bag. "The money is here. You can check it, if you like."

Clint wanted to seem as if he trusted Seagrave as much as the man trusted him.

"That's all right," he said. "I trust you."

"And I you, although I don't really know why. You can take this money back to the Kennelworth bank."

Clint recalled seeing the empty bank bag in Ed's room.

"I have their money bag," he said. "I can put it back in there."

"Good," he said. "Are the police aware that he was a bank robber?"

"I don't know," Clint said.

"Haven't you spoken with them?"

"If I do that," Clint explained, "I probably won't be allowed to take that money back to Kennelworth, since I'm not a lawman."

"Would that be so bad?"

"The people there trusted me to do this," Clint lied. "I'd like to get it done."

"I understand," Seagrave said. "Will the police be coming here?"

"It's not likely."

"If they do, what should I tell them?" the bank manager asked.

"The truth," Clint said. "Don't cause any trouble for yourself."

Clint picked the bag up off the desk.

"How will I know you got this money back to the rightful bank?" Seagrave asked.

"I'll send you a telegram as soon as I arrive in Kennelworth."

"That'll be very good," Seagrave said. "I'll be waiting for that." He stuck out his hand to shake. "Thank you, Mr. Adams. You may have saved me some embarrassment with my bank examiners."

"I'm happy I could do it, Mr. Seagrave," Clint said, and left.

Chapter Thirty

Clint returned to Ed and Dave's hotel only to retrieve the Kennelworth bank bag. He hoped he wouldn't run into any policemen.

As he passed the front desk on the way out the desk clerk asked him, "Sir, since Mr. Smith is dead, I assume his room is now available, but what about his friend. Do you know if he'll be coming back?"

"I didn't know what the police are going to do with him," Clint said. "But I can't be concerned about that. I'm leaving town."

And what do I do if the police come back here?" the clerk asked.

"You tell them the truth," Clint said. "Don't do anything to get yourself in trouble."

"Yes, Sir, will do."

Clint went to the livery stable where he had stashed his Tobiano. He saddled the horse himself, tossed his saddlebags over the saddle, and mounted up. He was in a hurry to get out of Fort Collins before the police came looking for him. He was willing to let them do whatever they wanted with Jack. His concern now was only to get the money back to Kennelworth, Utah Territory.

***

He was able to cut good time off the days it took him to cover the 550 miles from Kennelworth to Fort Collins. When he rode into town he attracted a lot of attention. Apparently, much of the populace expected that he would never return.

Clint was tired from pushing, and so was the Tobiano. He rode directly to Finch's livery. The big man greeted him with a huge smile, and a matching hug.

"I knew you'd be back," Finch said. "Did you catch them?"

"I tracked them to Fort Collins. Ed drank too much and got himself killed. Jack was picked up by the police to identify Ed's body."

"Did they arrest him?"

"I don't know what they would have arrested him for."

"So you think they'll let him go?"

"Probably."

"And the money?"

"It's in my saddlebags," Clint said. "But who do I give it to?"

"Well, the bank is closed, they don't have a new bank manager."

"Is Sills still here?"

"Yeah, and still sheriff," Finch said.

"I can't give the money to him," Clint said. "It'd be too big a temptation. What about the Town Council?"

"That makes more sense," Finch said. "I can call a meetin'."

"Do that. I'm going to check back into my hotel, freshen up and get something to eat."

"And the money?"

"I'll have it with me the entire time."

"That's takin' a chance," Finch said. "You were seen ridin' back into town."

"Why else would I come back other than to return the money?" Clint asked. "Do they still think I robbed the bank and killed the manager?"

"Probably not—not all of them, anyway. But that doesn't mean there won't be some idiot who wants to try and take the money from you. After you get cleaned up I'll meet you at Byron's Black & White Saloon. I'll bring some food from the Bellflower Café. I should've talked to some members of the council, by then."

"Okay," Clint said. "I'll see you there."

Clint left the Tobiano with Finch and headed for the same hotel he had stayed in before, the Cattleman's House.

"You're back, Mr. Adams," the clerk said.

"I'm back. Can I get the same room?"

"Sure thing." The clerk gave him his key. "Did you catch those two bank robbers?"

"I caught up to them," Clint said. "One's dead, and one was in custody when I left Fort Collins."

"You tracked them all the way to Colorado?"

"That I did."

"And I bet you got the money back."

"I did," Clint said.

"The bank's still closed," the clerk said. "Who you gonna give it to?"

"That's something I'll have to figure out."

"Maybe Miss Dawson?"

"We'll see," Clint said. "I'm going to clean up and then I'll be at the Black & White Saloon."

"Yes, Sir," the clerk said. "I'm just glad you're back."

Clint went up to his room.

***

Ken, the bartender in The Purple Heart Saloon, knocked on Minerva Dawson's door. She opened it and glared at him.

"This better be good," she said.

"It is," he told her. "Clint Adams just rode in."

Chapter Thirty-One

After Clint freshened up and changed his clothes, he walked to the Black and White Saloon. Finch's cousin, Byron, smiled broadly as he reached the bar. Clint kept his saddlebags on his shoulder.

"Finch said you'd be coming back," Byron said, placing a cold beer on the bar.

"Did you believe him?" Clint asked.

"Let's say I hoped," Byron said. "What about the men you were trackin'?"

"They won't be returning."

"Did you—"

"—kill them. No, I didn't, but one of them is dead. The other is in custody, but I don't know any more than that."

"And the bank money?"

Clint patted his saddlebags and said, "Right here." He looked around to see if anyone had heard him, but there were only a few customers seated out of earshot.

"All of it?"

"Every penny."

"What are you gonna do with it?" Byron asked. "The bank's still closed."

Clint picked up the beer and drank.

"Finch says he's going to call a meeting of the Town Council to decide what to do with the bank's money. He'll meet me here with some food from the Bellflower. I'm pretty hungry."

"Have you bothered to talk to the sheriff since you got back?"

"I've only been here about an hour. I don't know if there's any point in talking to him, though."

"He hardly comes out of his office," Byron said. "I'm hoping the Town Council will vote to replace him."

"Let's see what your cousin has to say when he gets here," Clint said.

"What about the purple lady?"

"I haven't heard her called that before."

"I call her that. I'm bettin' she'll be happy to see that money."

"I figured a lot of it must be hers."

"By now she probably heard you're back. You gonna stop in and see her?"

"Maybe," Clint said. "I haven't decided. I want to get rid of this money, first."

"I have a safe in the back. You can put it there."

"I've had it this long," Clint said, risking offending the man. "I'll hold on to it a little longer."

"I don't blame you," Byron said, "It must be a lot of money."

"Actually," Clint said, "it's not as much as I expected."

"Well," Byron said, "small town, small bank."

"I suppose." Clint turned and looked at the batwing doors. "Where's Finch? I'm getting hungry."

At that moment, the hostler walked in, carrying food on a tray.

"Sorry," he said, setting the tray on the bar. "Sandwiches was the best I could do."

"If they're from the Bellflower, they'll be good sandwiches," Byron said.

And they were. Clint and Finch ate the sandwiches at the bar with Byron.

"What happened with the Council?" Clint asked.

"With me, there are six," Finch said. "I spoke with three others. We think we can have a full meeting tonight. I'll try to get them to make some decisions."

"What about the mayor?" Clint asked.

"He'll be there."

"And the sheriff?"

"He doesn't usually attend. We all know he's useless."

"Then I suggest, after the Council decides what to do about the money, they get themselves a new sheriff."

"You're not volunteerin', are you?"
Clint laughed and said, "Not a chance."

Chapter Thirty-Two

"A couple of the Council members wanted to know if you'd attend," Finch told Clint. "I think they want to hear your story of recovering the money."

"What does it matter how I recovered it?" Clint asked. "I did."

"Curiosity."

"All right," Clint said. "I'll attend. Just tell me when and where."

"Where will you be?" Finch asked.

"Here, I guess," Clint said. "I feel secure, here."

"Byron will look after you," Finch said. "There's already been some talk around town of tryin' to take the money from you."

"And do what with it?"

"That's what we're meeting tonight to decide, ain't it?"

"I hope so," Clint said.

"Come on over to my livery at six-thirty, and we'll walk to the town hall together."

"Okay. See you then."

As Finch went out, Clint looked at Byron and asked, "Will you be at the meeting?"

"Not me," Byron said. "I hate politics. I like it right here behind my bar."

"I can't say I blame you."

"You gonna eat that last sandwich?" Byron asked.

"If you give me another beer, I'll split it with you."

"Deal," Byron said.

He drew another beer while Clint split the sandwich. His hands were full when three men walked in through the batwing doors.

"Just freeze right there, Gunsmith," one of them said.

Clint turned his head and looked at the three men. They all wore guns.

"What's on your mind, friend?" Clint asked, the sandwich falling from his hands onto the bar.

"Money, friend," the man said. "You've got it, and we want it."

"The money belongs to the bank."

"There ain't no bank anymore," the man said. His companions nodded their agreement.

"Then it belongs to the town," Clint said. "The Council will decide what to do with it tonight."

"Well, we've already decided what we want to do with it," the man said. "Is that it, on your shoulder?"

"Yes."

"Then drop it," the man said. "Or toss it to me."

"No chance on either count, my friend."

"Then we'll take it from you."

"Don't be a fool, Willie."

"You know this man?" Clint asked.

"I know the big mouth," Byron said. "His name's Willie Garvin."

"Mr. Garvin," Clint said, "take your friends and go."

"Not without those saddlebags," Garvin said. "There's no bank, my friend. That money belongs to whoever can take it."

"Well, that's not going to be you."

"Get out, Willie," Byron said.

Willie thought it over, and then said, "I gotta try."

Apparently, his friends agreed with him, as he went for his gun, they went for theirs, as well.

Clint's hand flashed for his gun, he fired three times, with perfect precision. Each man caught a bullet in their chest, which pierced their hearts. Two of them fell to the floor, and Willie's bullet drove him back through the batwing doors, to fall dead in the street.

"Damn it!" Clint cursed.

"You gave them every chance," Byron said.

Clint turned to the other customers, who were standing by their tables.

"You all saw that?"

"Yeah," one man said.

"They went for their guns, first," another said.

Clint replaced live rounds into his gun, and then holstered it.

"What do we do with them, now?" he asked.

"Let's just toss them out into the street," Byron suggested.

Clint actually gave that some thought, then said, "No." He looked at the other three men in the place. "Will you help me get them to the undertaker?"

"Sure," one of them said, and they all came forward.

***

It took some doing, but when they all returned to the Black & White Clint said to Byron, "Give them drinks on me."

The three men bellied up to the bar and Byron served four beers.

"You still gonna wait here until the Council meets?" Byron asked Clint.

"I've got nothing else to do," Clint said.

Byron put his hand beneath the bar and came out holding something.

"I got a deck of cards."

Chapter Thirty-Three

After Clint left the Black & White he walked to the livery.

"All set?" he asked Finch.

The hostler turned to face him, wiping his hands on a rag.

"First let me clean up."

While he was waiting, Clint went to check and see how Toby was.

"Hey, big boy," he said, entering the stall. He stroked the animal's neck. "You getting some rest? Enough to eat? Finch being good to you?"

He walked around, checked all over, and found him in fine condition. As he came out of the stall, Finch reappeared, wearing a clean jacket.

"Are you ready?"

Clint tapped the saddlebags on his shoulder and said, "Ready."

They left the livery and started to walk.

"I heard what happened this afternoon," Finch said. "You impressed Byron."

"I wasn't looking to impress anyone," Clint said. "I was just trying to stay alive."

"And you did a good job."

"Tell me, is Minerva going to be at this meeting?"

"Yes. All of the Council members will be there, and that includes her."

"That could solve the whole problem."

"How do you mean?"

"I could just hand the money to her," Clint said.

"I don't think the other members of the Council would agree to that."

"Oh. I thought she ruled with an iron hand."

"She has, for a long time, but I think things are changing."

"Will she allow that?"

"I don't think she'll have a choice."

"What's going to make a bunch of men who have been frightened by her for years suddenly change their minds?" Clint asked.

"Maybe meeting a man who isn't frightened will do it," Finch said.

"I guess we'll see."

It was dusk when they reached City Hall. The front door was unlocked, so Clint just followed Finch in.

"I haven't known many hostlers who sit on Town Councils," Clint commented.

"I own more than a livery stable," Finch said.

"I thought that might be it."

They walked the first floor hall of the two-story building til they reached a solid oak door. It was also unlocked, and they walked in.

There were six people seated at a long, wooden table that had been waxed to a reflective shine.

"Gentlemen," Finch said, "meet Clint Adams. Miss Dawson already knows him."

"Do we all need to be introduced?" a while-haired man asked.

"No, Mr. Mayor," Clint said before anyone else could respond. "It's not necessary. I understand you people make decisions for the town."

"Some of us more than others," Minerva Dawson said.

"Yes, yes, Minerva," the man who spoke said, "we all know your position." He looked at Clint and said, "Would you have a seat?" Finch had already taken his normal place at the table.

"Thanks." Clint sat and kept the saddlebags on his lap.

"Is that the money?" the man asked Clint.

"It is."

"And the bank robbers?"

"You mean you no longer think I robbed the bank?"

"You'd hardly rob the bank, and kill the manager, and then come back with the money."

"Who says he's returned with *all* the money?" Minerva asked.

"That's a good question," Clint said. "Do any of you know just how much was taken from the bank?"

The mayor said, "We had a bank examiner in here last week. He went over the accounts and came up with a number."

"And our mayor is the only one who knows it," Minerva said, "but of course, I know how much I had in the bank."

All the men at the table wrinkled up their faces as Clint said, "I see."

"So," the mayor said, "you tell us how much you brought back, and we'll see if the numbers match."

"All I can say," Clint patted the saddlebags, "that is what they had when I caught up to them."

"You mean, minus what they spent," the mayor asked.

"I mean they could have buried some of the money somewhere, to be recovered later."

"You think that's what they did? Finch asked.

"No, I don't," Clint said. "I pretty much found all their campsites. I think they kept all the money with them to split later."

"You mean, they hadn't split it, yet?" Minerva asked.

"I don't think they even counted it until they got to Fort Collins. And then I don't think Ed told Jack how much it was. I'm assuming he intended to kill Jack and keep it all."

"Is that what Ed did?" Minerva asked. "Kill Jack?"

"No," Clint said, "he never got the chance. It was Ed who was killed in the street by a couple of robbers."

"Jesus," one of the other men said, speaking for the first time.

"And what happened to the other one?" Minerva asked. "Jack?"

"He was in police custody when I left," Clint said.

"Under arrest?" the mayor asked.

Clint shook his head.

"They took him to identify the body."

"And then what?" Minerva asked.

"I don't know," Clint said. "I left town. But I don't think Jack will come anywhere near here again."

"Very well," the mayor said. "So how much is it, Mr. Adams?"

Clint stood up, opened both saddlebags and dumped the money on the table.

"I counted it this afternoon," Clint said. "It's thirty-one thousand, one hundred and eighty dollars."

They all digested that number, and then the mayor asked, "That's all?"

Chapter Thirty-Four

"That's what I said when I found the money," Clint said. "I thought a bank job would have yielded more."

"That depends," Minerva said.

"On what?" Clint asked.

"On how much faith a town has in its bank."

"And?"

"This town didn't have much."

"So thirty-one thousand, one hundred and eighty dollars doesn't surprise you?"

"No,"

"Wait a minute," the mayor said. "We only have Adams' word that this is the entire take from the bank job."

"Do you want to call him a liar, Mr. Mayor?" Finch asked.

"Well, uh, no . . ."

"Then that's settled," Finch said. "This is all the money that was taken from the bank. Now the question is, what do we do with it?"

"And I don't need to be here for that, do I?" Clint asked. "Where this money goes once I turn it over doesn't really concern me."

"And since none of my money was in the bank," Minerva said, standing, "it doesn't concern me, either. Clint, would you escort me back to The Purple Heart?" she asked, while pulling on her purple gloves.

"It'd be my pleasure," Clint said.

"Hold on, please," the mayor said, before they could leave. "We have one more thing on the agenda. We need a new sheriff."

"Have an election," Clint said. "That's what most town's do."

"Yes, yes," the man said, "but we need to replace Sills until we can arrange one."

"What's that got to do with me?" Clint said, playing dumb.

"We would like to offer you the job, Mr. Adams," the mayor said.

"This town was ready to hang me a little while ago."

"We realize our mistake," the mayor said. "We feel you would be perfect for the job."

"I'm afraid I'm not interested," Clint said. He extended his arm and said to Minerva, "Miss Dawson?"

As they left the room Finch asked, "Don't anybody think we should have thanked Mr. Adams for bringin' this money back?"

***

As they strolled back through town Minerva asked, "How much longer do you intend to stay?"

"Not too long," he said. "I'm back where I started when I first rode in, wanting to get some rest for me and my horse."

"Are you staying at the Cattleman?"

"Yes."

"And where will you be drinking?"

"Probably at the Black and White."

"And gambling?"

"Well, that's a different matter," Clint said. "There's not much gambling at the Black and White."

They stopped in front of The Purple Heart.

"You're welcome to gamble here," she said.

"I'll keep that in mind," he said.

She stepped up onto the boardwalk and entered The Purple Heart. For a moment he considered following her, but eventually walked on.

***

Inside, Minerva stopped at the bar. Ken came rushing over.

"How did it go?"

"He returned the money, but didn't accept the job of sheriff," she replied.

"And what about the bank?" Ken asked. "They gonna reopen it?"

"I left before they decided that."

"Whataya think?"

"To tell you the truth," she said, "it doesn't matter to me, at all. My money was never in there. If Mr. Adams shows up, let him come up."

"Still think you'll get him to pay for your time?" Ken asked.

"Who knows?

As Minerva headed for the stairs, Tammy walked into the saloon.

"What's going on?" she asked Ken.

"Clint Adams is back," he told her. "He brought the bank money with him."

"That's great," she said.

Ken shrugged.

"For some people."

"Hey, I had a hundred dollars in there. Will I get it back?"

"That's what they're tryin' to decide."

"I better get dressed," she said, but as she started away she stopped and turned back. "What hotel is Mr. Adams in?"

"The Cattleman. Why?"

"Just curious."

She went to get ready for work.

Chapter Thirty-Five

From The Purple Heart Saloon, Clint went back to the Black & White Saloon, rather than while away the time in his room. But as of late, talking to Byron and, later, to Finch started to get tiresome. Finch said the Council hadn't made any decisions and were going to meet again the next day.

"We'll come to some decisions, then," he assured Clint.

"I hope you do," Clint said, "but to tell you the truth, I don't really care."

He said good night to the cousins, and headed for his hotel.

***

He was in his room for about three hours when there was a knock on his door. He drew his gun from the holster hanging on the bedpost and padded barefoot across the floor.

"Who is it?" he asked.

"It's Tammy," she said. "Remember? From The Purple Heart Saloon?"

He opened the door slowly and peered out. There was no way he could know whether or not Minerva Dawson has sent the girl, to get him to open his door. But she was alone in the hall. She smiled at him.

"Hello," she said. "Can I come in?"

"Why not?"

He opened the door wide to admit her. She was wearing a shawl over her saloon dress, which was yellow. Clint closed the door and turned to return his gun to its holster.

"So you're not gonna shoot me?" she asked.

"I don't shoot pretty young girls," he told her. "What's on your mind, Tammy?"

"I thought you might like some company, tonight," she said.

"If Minerva sent you over here, she should have told that I don't pay for sex."

"Well, first, Minerva doesn't know I'm here," Tammy said, "and second, I didn't come here for money."

"Then why are you here?"

"I told you," she said. "I thought you might enjoy some company."

"Well, that's a nice idea—"

"I also heard that you brought all the bank's money back," Tammy told him. "I thought somebody should reward you for doing that."

"Why you?"

"I had a hundred dollars in the bank."

"Well, I'll try to make sure you get it back. Will you be all right walking home?"

"I'd be fine," she said, "but I'll be even better spending the night here." She tossed her shawl aside, then reached behind her to undo her dress and allow it to drop to the floor. "Free of charge, of course. You see, I'm a saloon girl, not a whore."

She was stark naked and so young her skin was perfect—smooth and unmarked. Her breasts were small, but round and solid, with pink nipples.

"I'm sorry," he said, "I didn't mean to imply—"

"That's okay," she said, interrupting him, "I'm sure people are always misjudging you, based on your reputation."

"All the time."

"So let's get your clothes off and just make friends. I'm not looking for anything more than that."

"That's fair."

Since his boots were already off, it didn't take long for Clint to discard the remains of his clothes. When he was naked they both liked what they saw. Coming together, they tumbled to the bed.

Chapter Thirty-Six

She was young, energetic and eager, so after a few minutes of rolling about on the bed together, she wrestled her way to the top. With a quick jerk of her hips she took Clint's penis inside. She was hot and wet and he sank deep inside her. She started to bounce up and down on him, and he realized just how young she was as he tried to match her rhythm.

She pressed her hands down flat on his chest, closed her eyes and tried to move her hips even faster. Clint thought for sure this girl was going to break his back . . .

****

Clint was still trying to catch his breath when Tammy, using her hands, made it clear she was ready for more.

"Hold on there," he said, pushing her hands away, "you're a lot younger than I am. I need a few minutes."

She pouted and asked, "How many is a few?" She stroked his cock, which reacted immediately. "It looks to me like you don't need no time, at all."

"Jesus," he said, as she closed her fist around him.

"I tell you what," she said. "You just lie back and relax and let me do the work.

That said, she shinnied down, got comfortable between his wide-spread legs, and took his cock into her eager mouth . . .

***

Minerva Dawson came down as it was nearing closing time.

"Where's Tammy?" she asked, looking around.

"She said she was taking the rest of the night off," Ken told her.

"She's making her own hours, now?" Minerva said. "That girl's got to learn a lesson or two."

"You gonna fire 'er?" Ken asked.

"No," Minerva said, "she's too damn popular for that. I doubt she took the night off for nothing." She saw the look on Ken's face. "Come on, Ken, where'd she go?"

"You want me to guess?"

"Would it be an educated guess?"

"Pretty much."

"Then make it."

"I think she went to Clint Adams' hotel."

"What for?" she asked, even though she knew it was a stupid question.

"To make him more comfortable, I guess."

"She's a child."

"Hey, you hired her."

"I was going to help her grow up," Minerva said. "I guess she's doing that herself."

She turned and headed for the stairs as the saloon emptied out.

"You want me to send her up when she gets back?" Ken called to her.

"That won't be til tomorrow morning, and by then the damage will be done. No, I'll see Adams before I see her."

"If you say so."

***

Clint did his best to keep up with the young girl, but he also thought he was going to swear off the young ones. Minerva Dawson would have been more his style, had she not insisted on being paid.

"What's wrong with whores?" Tammy asked.

"Nothing," he said. "Some of my best friends are whores. I just don't pay for sex."

They were lying side-by-side, and Clint was satisfied to hear the girl trying to catch her breath.

She laughed and said, "That's because you don't have to."

"What keeps you from being a whore?" he asked.

"That's easy," she said. "Smelly men. As a saloon girl I can pick and choose. As a whore I'd be working for money. That would mean I can't pick and choose."

"Like you chose me?"

"Exactly."

"It's nice to know I'm not smelly."

"Not at all," she said. "I noticed that about you, right off."

"Even in the middle of a smoke filled saloon?"

"Oh yes," she said, smiling. "I have a wonderful sense of smell."

"And you smell wonderful."

She propped herself up on an elbow, leaned over him, said, "Thank you, sir," and kissed him.

***

Finch entered the Black & White Saloon. By the time he got to the bar, Byron had a beer waiting for him.

"So? What's the verdict?" his cousin asked.

"Nothing decided tonight," Finch said. "We're meetin' again tomorrow."

"With or without the Gunsmith?"

"Without, this time."

Byron leaned on the bar and lowered his voice.

"How much did he bring back?"

"Apparently, all of it," Finch said.

"And how much was that?"

"About thirty-one thousand."

"That's all?" Byron asked. "From a bank vault?"

"Looks like Minerva keeps her money under her mattress," Finch said. "That might've doubled or tripled it."

"Well, that would make it easier than robbin' the bank," Byron said.

"I don't know about that," Finch said. "Those two idiots didn't make it look so hard."

"Well, even if she has it in a safe, and not under her mattress, we should be able to get at it. When do you want to do it?"

"I wanted to do it a long time ago and be away from here," Finch said. "Now I think we have to wait a bit longer."

"Wait for what?"

"For the Gunsmith to get out of town."

"Yeah," Byron said, "we don't wanna have to deal with him, do we?"

Chapter Thirty-Seven

The next morning Finch met with the rest of the Town Council and the decision was made to reopen the bank, and re-deposit the recovered money. The bank records were intact, so depositors would have access to their money. They would be allowed to let the funds remain on deposit, or withdraw them. When the question of a new sheriff came up, Finch advised bringing it up at another time. He said he thought reopening the bank was the most important thing.

With that decision made, it became necessary to name a new bank manager. Finch had a man in mind the whole time and when no one else came up with anyone, he named him.

"Andy Redmann?" the mayor repeated. "The only qualifications I can see is that he spends most days sitting in your cousin's saloon."

"And the bank manager's job is mostly sittin'." Finch said. "Anybody else got a candidate?"

Nobody did.

"Mr. mayor?" he said.

The man threw his hands up and said, "Fine. Andy Redmann is the new bank manager."

"Good," Finch said. "Let's get the money back into the safe."

"It's in the safe in my office," the mayor said. "It hasn't left this building since Adams dumped it out on the table."

"Somebody needs to take it over there safely," Finch said. "I nominate Clint Adams."

"If he's still in town," the mayor said.

"Don't worry about that," Finch said. "He is."

***

Clint remained in bed the next morning, watching Tammy dress.

"Tammy," he said, "don't come here again."

Fully covered, she turned and asked, "Why?"

"Because if I have to try to keep up with you again," he said, "I'll have a heart attack."

She laughed.

"I think I have more confidence in you than you do," she said.

"Did she send you here?" he asked.

"Minerva?" Tammy asked, "No, not at all. She doesn't like to share her men."

"I'm not her man," he pointed out.

"And now that I've been with you, you never will be. You're welcome. But she probably still has a use for you in mind, so you'll see her again."

"And what's she going to do to you for coming here?"

"She'll probably punish me," the girl said, "but I think it was worth it." She opened the door, said, "I'll see you soon," and left the room.

Clint left the bed, went to the pitcher-and-basin on the dresser and washed up. He dressed in the same jeans, but clean shirt, pulled on his boots, strapped on his holster, and went down to the lobby. It was empty but for the desk clerk.

"I hope you're not mad, Mr. Adams," the clerk said. "She told me it would be all right."

"It was," Clint said, "this time. But don't let her, or anyone else, for that matter, pass again. Understand?"

"Yessir," the young man said, "I understand."

Clint headed for the front door.

"Where are you off to, sir?" the clerk called, "if anyone should ask."

"If anyone asks," Clint said, "you don't have any idea where I am."

"Actually," the clerk said, "I don't."

Clint smiled.

"And let's keep it that way."

Chapter Thirty-Eight

Clint didn't know when the money would be returned to the bank, or when—and if—the bank would reopen. He assumed Finch would have those answers, but he wasn't sure about Finch, any longer. The man had presented himself as a hostler, running his livery stable, but Clint had never before seen a hostler sitting on the Town Council, let alone sitting at the head. Clint felt that Finch had the Council under his thumb, including the mayor. He wasn't sure, but he thought he knew someone who wouldn't be.

He just hoped he wouldn't have to pay for the information . . .

***

When the bartender Ken saw Clint Adams walk through the batwing doors of The Purple Heart Saloon he shook his head. How did she always know when they would come back?

"The boss lady says you should just come on up," Ken said.

"I'll have a beer, first."

"Comin' up." Ken drew the beer and set it on the bar. "On the house."

"Why's that?" Clint asked, picking up the beer.

"Hey, she's the boss. Whatever she says goes."

"I get that," Clint said. "Tell me something, Ken."

"What's that?"

"How long has Minerva been on the Town Council?"

"She got herself a spot as soon as she opened this place," Ken said. "Why ask?"

"I thought when I attended, I'd see Minerva taking charge. Instead, I saw her say very little while the hostler, Finch, took charge. Even over the mayor. Why would that be?"

"The mayor knows his days are numbered," the bartender said. "Kennelworth is gonna have a new mayor and new sheriff."

"When?"

"The boss figures there'll be an election within the next six months."

Clint finished his beer but before he went upstairs he asked, "Is Minerva going to run for mayor?"

"I doubt it," Ken said. "I don't think this town would elect a woman."

"But Minerva commands a lot of respect here, doesn't she?"

"Fear," Ken said, "she deals in fear."

"Why's the town afraid of her?"

"She knows a lot of secrets."

"And she can't use those secrets to get herself elected mayor?"

"She might," Ken said, "if she chose to."

"But you don't think she'd do that?"

"No, I don't think she would."

Clint turned and started across the floor to the stairs.

***

Tammy was in Minerva's room, being called on the carpet.

"If you want to keep working here, little girl, you won't be making your own decisions. You'll wait until I tell you what to do."

Since Tammy was still willing to work for Minerva, she simply said, "Yes, Ma'am."

"So go get ready for your shift."

Tammy nodded and went out the door. Just at that moment, Clint appeared at the top of the stairs.

"Are you in trouble?" he asked her.

"I don't know," she replied with a smile, "maybe you are."

He laughed and said, "We'll see."

"I'll talk to you later," she said, "away from here."

He nodded and as she walked off down the hall, he approached Minerva's door and knocked.

"Come!"

Clint opened the door and entered. Minerva was sitting in front of her mirror, wearing a robe and working on her make-up. She looked at him in the mirror.

"What do you want?"

"I have some questions."

"Do you mind if I continue to fix my face?" she asked.

"Not at all."

"Then go ahead and ask."

"Who holds the top position on the Town Council?"

"You couldn't tell?"

"It looked like Finch, but I've never seen a hostler holding that spot in any town."

"You must know by now that this isn't a normal town," she said.

"Well, I've never seen a town under the thumb of a woman," he replied.

"So why am I not at the head of the Council?"

"I was wondering that."

"It's simple," she said. "I don't want to be."

"And Finch?"

"Oh, he wanted it from the beginning. Also, pretty much whatever businesses in town I don't own, he does."

"Then what's he doing working in a livery stable?

"That's easy. He likes it, and he owns it."

"Does he own the Black and White Saloon."

"No, that's his cousin Byron's."

"But they must be partners."

"In some businesses, yes. But the saloon in Byron's and the livery stable is Finch's."

"And the bank?"

"That was always considered to be owned and run by the town."

"And do you know where the money is now?"

"Until the new bank manager actually takes over and the bank opens again, it's in the mayor's safe."

"And you, Finch and the others trust the mayor?"

"We need a new mayor for the same season we need a new sheriff."

"No guts?"

"Exactly," she said.

"Then why were they hired?"

"Some of us thought they'd be easier to handle," she said, "Now it seems like we need more courage in those offices."

"And you're happy with your standing?"

She smiled.

"Don't you think a woman enjoys being feared?" she asked him.

"I don't know about other women," he said, "but I'm sure you do."

She smiled again, stood up and dropped her robe to the floor. She was completely naked.

"Are sure you don't want to leave some money on my dresser, now?" she asked.

"I'm positive."

He turned and left her standing there, naked and annoyed.

Chapter Thirty-Nine

He had returned the money. Why did he care where it was? The mayor's safe might be more secure than reopening the bank. That is, unless the mayor planned on stealing it. And even if he did, why should he care? Minerva Dawson had tried and tried to play him, and now he knew that Finch had been playing him since he got there.

It seemed Finch wanted him to think Minerva was running things when it was now more likely that he and his cousin, Byron, were in charge. Clint didn't like having the wool pulled over his eyes. All he wanted now was to get this over with.

***

Stopping in to see Minerva had kept Clint from having breakfast. He found a small café he hadn't been in before and decided to eat there. He was intending for it to be his last meal in Kennelworth.

***

After lunch Clint decided to get it over with and walked to Finch's livery stable. Finch was working on shoeing a horse.

"Clint," he said. "I'm doin' all four, but I'll be with you in a little while. Wanna wait?"

"Sure, but I'll wait at the Black and While."

"Tell Byron to give you what you want, on me."

"Thanks, I'll see you there."

Clint figured he'd just as soon talk to Byron as Finch. He figured the two were a pair.

"You're still in town," Byron said, as Clint came up to the bar.

"I told Finch I'd meet him here."

"And he said whatever you wanted was on the house."

"You got it."

"Beer?"

"That's fine."

Byron drew a cold one and set it down in front of Clint. He looked around, saw two men sitting at their own table. He recognized them from every other time he had been in there. Both were wearing a gun.

"I get it now," Clint said.

"Get what?" Byron asked.

"Those two," Clint said. "They're always here?"

"They like it here," Byron said.

"Sure," Clint said, "they get paid to like it."

"What's your point?"

"You and your cousin need dirty work done," Clint said. "These fellas do it?"

"Finch and me, we can pretty well do whatever dirty work needs to be done."

"It's always good to have somebody watch your back," Clint said.

"That's what cousins are for," Byron said, folding his arms and leaning back. "You sound like a man with somethin' on his mind."

"I do," Clint said, "but I'll wait for Finch to get here so I can give it to you both."

"You better have another beer, then," Byron said.

"Thanks."

Byron set another one down in front of Clint.

"Have you seen Minerva Dawson today?" Byron asked.

"This morning," Clint said.

"To say goodbye?"

"Not exactly," Clint said. "We won't miss each other when I leave."

"And when's that gonna be?" Byron asked.

Clint picked up his fresh beer, took a drink and said, "Any minute now."

Chapter Forty

Finch came in about twenty minutes and another beer later.

"Sorry it took me so long," he said, joining Clint at the bar.

"That's okay," Clint said. "Your cousin kept me entertained."

"Clint's got something on his mind, Finch," Byron said.

"Oh?" Finch asked. "What's that?"

"I don't like how the people in this town have been trying to use me."

"Who's tried to use you except for the two bank robbers?" Finch asked.

"Who hasn't?" Clint asked. "You, Byron, Minerva. You tell me. Anyone else? The whole Town Council?"

"Clint, I didn't expect the Gunsmith to sound like such a victim."

"Why not? That's what you've all been trying to make me since I got here," Clint said. "I may not be a victim, but I've pretty much been a fool."

"Don't be so hard on yourself, Clint," Finch said. "Why consider yourself a fool?"

"Because admitting it is going to keep me from let-ting anyone ever make a fool out of me again."

"Maybe you had that experience with Minerva," Finch said, looking amused, "but that's not somethin' I'd try."

"You're trying it again, right now, Finch," Clint said. "It's not going to work, this time."

Finch looked at Byron, who looked past Clint, who knew he could only be looking as his two men. Then the cousins exchanged a look.

"Tell Byron to take it easy, Finch," Clint said. "If those men behind me draw their guns, somebody's going to die."

"Nobody deserves to die, Clint," Finch said. "There's no reason for it. Okay, we used you, but that was to get the money back from the bank job."

"And who was behind the bank job?" Clint asked.

Finch and Byron exchanged another look.

"Clint," Finch said, "we appreciate what you did, bringin' that money back. We're gonna be makin' some changes here in town, but we don't need to have you here, anymore."

"So you want me to leave?"

"The sooner the better," Byron said.

"You fellas aren't that friendly, anymore."

"Well," Finch said, "for a while I thought you might help this town get out from under Minerva Dawson's purple gloves, but I think we're ready to do that ourselves."

Clint found himself wondering what they were going to do to make that happen?

"Another beer?" Finch asked.

"I don't think so," Clint said. "And I think I'll pay for these." He dropped the money on the bar.

"Suit yourself," Byron said, picking it up.

"I guess you'll be leavin'," Finch said.

"First thing in the morning," Clint said.

"I'll have your horse ready," Finch promised.

Clint nodded and left.

***

He went to his hotel and paid his bill, so he wouldn't have to stop in the morning. After that he went to his room, wishing it was already morning. He'd had enough of Kennelworth, and was willing to leave them all to themselves. Finch and his cousin would probably be battling each other for control. As far as Clint was concerned, good luck to them all. They deserved each other.

He turned in early so he could get an early start in the morning . . .

***

He was asleep a few hours when somebody pounded on his door. He came instantly awake, grabbed his gun from the bedpost and went to the door.

"Who is it?"

"Frank Sills! Lemme in, Adams."

"Are you alone?" Clint asked.

"Yeah, yeah, I'm alone!"

Clint cracked the door and saw Sills in the hall. He was alone and looked scared stiff.

"Come in," Clint said, opening the door.

Sills hurried into the room.

"You gotta help me, Adams," he said.

"What's going in?" Clint asked, still holding his gun. Sills was wearing his gun, but he was acting like he'd forgotten it.

"Somebody tried to kill me."

"When?"

"About fifteen minutes ago," Sills said. "I was asleep in one of my cells and somebody took a shot at me. I ran."

"Here?"

"I didn't know where else to go," Sills said.

"Who do you think wants you dead?"

"I have no idea," Sills said. He rubbed his face with both hands. "You got a drink?"

"No, sorry," Clint said. He thought about holstering his gun, but decided against it.

"What are you really doing here, Sheriff? And where's your badge?"

Sills hesitated, then said, "I ain't the sheriff anymore."

"You quit?"

Sills shook his head.

"I got fired."

"If you're not the law anymore, why would somebody try to kill you?"

"I don't know." Sills still looked nervous.

"You say you were in your office when it happened?" Clint asked.

"That's right," Sills said, looking away.

"What were you doing there if you got fired?" Clint asked.

"I was packin' up my things."

"The office is across the street."

"So?"

"I didn't hear the shot."

"You were probably asleep."

"That's not likely," Clint said. "Sleeping that soundly could get me killed. I think you better leave, Sills. Tell whoever sent you it didn't work."

"I don't know what you're talkin' about," Sills said. "If you're not gonna help me, I'll just leave."

"You do that."

Sills hesitated, then rushed to the door and left. Clint was sure he had been sent to his room to kill him. What he didn't know was why? He wasn't a danger to anyone, as he had already announced his departure. Apparently, the fact that he was leaving wasn't good enough for someone.

Before going back to sleep Clint took precautions to barricade the door to his room.

Chapter Forty-One

Clint wanted nothing more than to leave Kennelworth that next morning, but he also wanted to know who would be stupid enough to send Frank Sills to kill him? The cousins? Minerva Dawson? The man obviously didn't have it in him. Clint thought maybe he should have pressed him. He decided to look for Sills before he did anything else. He didn't know where else to look, so he went to the sheriff's office. He found the man sitting at the desk with a knife sticking out of his back. He wasn't wearing a badge. Clint searched the drawers of the desk, found no sign of the star. He figured if he could find whoever was wearing the badge now, he might find the killer.

He left the body where it was, slumped over the desk, and headed for the livery stable. True to his word Finch had the Tobiano saddled and ready.

"I thought you'd be here earlier," the hostler said.

"So did I," Clint said, "but I had another stop to make."

"Where?"

"The sheriff's office."

"What for?" Finch said. "We took Sill's badge from him, yesterday. We ain't replaced him, yet."

"Sills told me that last night when somebody sent him to my room to kill me."

"What? He tried to kill you?" Finch blurted.

"He didn't have the nerve to try it."

"Did he tell you who sent 'im?" Finch asked.

"No, he just ran out," Clint said. "I should've pressed him last night, and now he's dead."

"I don't understand who'd kill 'im," Finch said, seemingly surprised. "He was no danger to anyone."

"Well, somebody wanted him dead," Clint said.

"It wasn't me," Finch said. "Byron and me, we were happy to just take his badge,"

"Who are you going to replace him with?"

"We don't know yet," Finch said. "The Town Council's gonna discuss it. What's it to you, anyway? I thought you were leaving today."

"I was," Clint said, "but apparently that wasn't good enough for somebody."

"You really think somebody sent Sills to kill you?"

"Maybe it was a test," Clint said, "and he failed."

"So somebody killed him because he didn't kill you?" Finch asked.

"Could be."

"Well, don't look at me, or anyone on the Council, for that matter," Finch said. "We're satisfied with you leavin' town. Especially after you did us a good turn. What reason would we have to kill you?"

"I don't like leaving with a target on my back," Clint said.

"Ain't that the way you live your life?" Finch asked.

"I guess you're right about that," Clint agreed.

"So you'll pull out?" Finch asked.

"I reckon I will, Finch," Clint said. "I reckon I've had just about enough of Kennelworth."

Clint took the Tobiano's reins from Finch and walked him outside. The hostler watched from the livery door while Clint mounted up and headed out of town.

Once he figured he was out of sight he reined in, dismounted and checked the saddle to be sure it was cinched in nice and tight. There was always the chance Finch had rigged the saddle to slip and dump Clint on his ass. Or worse, his head. But it seemed all right. Apparently, Finch was telling the truth about wanting Clint out of town. There was probably no one out there with a rife waiting for Clint's saddle to slip.

He mounted up again and considered his options . . .

***

As Clint rode away Byron came out from the back of the livery.

"He gone?" he asked.

"Yeah," Finch said, "but he found Sills."

"And he's still leavin'?"

"He's had enough of this town," Finch said.

"I have, too," Byron said. "Maybe we should just leave it to Minerva."

"You can do that," Finch said. "I've got too much invested here."

He turned and went back inside.

Chapter Forty-Two

Clint found a safe place to leave the Tobiano tied to a tree, and made his way back to town on foot. He wanted to see what was going on with Sills dead.

He made his way back to the livery in time to see Byron leaving and Finch going back inside. He wondered what was being done about Sills' body?

He watched the livery for about twenty minutes, waiting to see Finch leave. When he finally did Clint followed the hostler to the sheriff's office. Glancing in the front window he saw Sills' body still at the desk. Finch wasn't paying it any attention. He was searching the office for something, perhaps the sheriff's badge.

As he continued to watch he saw that he was right. Finch managed to locate the sheriff's badge, and stuck it in his pocket. Clint didn't understand how he had missed it.

While he watched as Finch was leaving the office, Clint heard others approaching. He assumed Byron had returned to the Black & White and sent his two gunmen to the office.

He was caught in between . . .

***

Finch opened the office door as the two men approached.

"What took you so long?"

"Come on, Finch," one of them said. "We came as soon as Byron told us."

"What's this about?" the other man asked, indicating the body of Sills slumped over the desk.

"He was expendable," Finch said.

"What's that mean?" one of them asked.

"It means he was a waste of time," Finch said.

"Who you gonna replace him with?"

"One of you, if you want it," Finch said, holding the badge up.

"For how long?"

"The Town Council will decide that."

"How much is the pay?"

"Forty a month."

"A house?"

"No," Finch said, "you'll sleep in one of the cells."

The two men exchanged a look, and then one said, "I'll take it, for a while, anyway."

Finch handed him the badge and said, "Congratulations Sheriff Holton."

***

Clint found an alley to hide in before Finch opened the door to let them in. He heard the whole conversation, including Finch hiring the new sheriff. He stayed in the alley until the two men left to go back to the Black & White.

Clint decided to face Finch instead of giving him time to get rid of Sills' body.

Clint opened the door and darted in, gun in hand. Finch was wearing a gun in a holster, but didn't look comfortable with it.

"Don't go for that gun, Finch," Clint said.

"I'd never draw against you, Adams."

"But you'd send an idiot like Sills after me."

Finch shrugged and said, "I figured I made out either way."

"Why do you want me dead?"

"I don't want you dead," Finch said, "but I don't lose either way."

"You lose if I kill you here and now," Clint said.

"I don't think you'd do that."

"Why not?"

"You've got no reason to," Finch said. "Just leave, Adams. I'll make sure no one follows you. If there's a target on your back, it won't be put there by me."

"What about Minerva?"

"If she puts a target on you, there's nothin' I can do about it."

"So you and she don't work together?"

"We have," Finch said. "But for the most part I have my business and she has hers."

"So why don't you put on the sheriff's badge, and make Minerva mayor?"

"No, I like it the way it is now, with Holton wearing the badge. As for Minerva, she's never wanted to be mayor."

"Fine," Clint said, "work it out between you."

"So you'll head out?" Finch asked.

"I'm already gone," Clint said.

They both looked at Sills' body.

"Don't worry," Finch said. "I'll take care of him."

"I'm not worried about him."

"I won't send anyone after you," Finch assured him, again.

"You better not," Clint said. "If you do, I'll kill them and then come back for you."

"Don't worry," Finch said, "if I wanted you dead, I don't think I have anybody who can do the job."

"Take my word for it," Clint said, "you don't."

Chapter Forty-Three

For months Clint Adams had not been liking the version of himself he was seeing. His time in Kennelworth had pushed him almost to the edge. He wanted to put this time behind him and start making some changes. He had been letting himself become involved in situations that really weren't his business. Once he was on his way, Kennelworth, or anywhere in Utah, for that matter, were going to be in his past.

His friend, John Locke, had a spread in Las Vegas, New Mexico. For a long time he was more Soldier of Fortune than anything else. But eventually he decided to buy a spread, and work it, and maybe take a job or two now and then to finance a new life. He had a man who, like Clint Adams, had no live with a reputation. Known as The Widowmaker—like The Gunsmith—he lived with a target on his back. Maybe, working the spread together, they could keep each other alive. He had been asking Clint to buy in with him, and they would work the ranch together, and watch each other's back. Clint was starting to see the sense in such a move.

All he had to do was mount up and ride south, leave this place and these people behind him.

He left Finch in the sheriff's office, with the man's body, and walked to where he had left the Tobiano. He untied the horse from the tree, and looked around. He was still expecting some kind of double-cross. He didn't trust anyone in Kennelworth to act on the up-and-up.

***

After Clint Adams left town—hopefully for real, this time—Finch left the former sheriff's body where it was, left the office and went to the Black & White Saloon.

"Is he gone?' Byron asked.

"Yeah."

"This time for good?"

"Don't worry," Finch said. "He's gone. Now we can get on with our plans for Kennelworth."

"Like changing the name?"

"First thing."

"And what about Minerva?" Byron asked.

"I think we've put up with her purple gloves long enough," Finch said.

"For a while I thought we were gonna have to deal with Adams on her behalf," Byron said.

"On her behalf, or against her?" Finch asked his cousin.

"Let's just say I'm glad he's gone," Byron said. "I didn't like when he rode into town. It was a complication we didn't need."

"As it turns out Clint did us a good turn, and now he's on his way."

"I hope you're right, cousin."

"I need help removing our former sheriff from his office."

"I'll take care of it."

"Good," Finch said, "that leaves me free to deal with Minerva."

"To do what?" Byron asked. "Kill 'er?"

"Let's hope not," Finch said. "Let's hope she makes the right decision."

Finch left the Black & White and headed for the Purple Heart.

***

When Ken, the bartender, saw Finch enter The Purple Heart, he knew something was up. To almost everyone else in the saloon, Finch was just the town hostler. So no one paid much attention to him.

"What brings you here, Finch?" Ken asked. "Other than a superior brand of beer."

"The beer at the Black and White is just fine," Finch said. "I'm here to talk to Minerva."

"About what?"

"The future of Kennelworth."

"Well," Ken said, "that is her main concern. Go on up, but be sure to knock."

"Thanks."

Finch crossed the crowded floor and went up the stairs.

"Come in," she called when he knocked.

As he opened the door and stepped in she shot him in the chest.

"Sorry, Finch," she said. "Without Clint Adams around I can't trust you."

"Don't—" he gagged, "don't kill Byron—"

As he slumped to the floor she said, "I don't think I have a choice."

She removed her robe, put on a simple dress that would hide the gun she stuck in her garter. A purple garter.

Before leaving the room she covered his body with a blanket. She pulled on her purple gloves and went downstairs to the bar.

"Was that a shot?" Ken asked her.

"Maybe."

"Where's Finch?"

"He won't be coming down."

"Ever?"

"Ever."

"So Byron's next?"

Yes."

"We're buyin' the Black and White?"

"Acquiring it," she corrected.

"Why're you doin' this yourself?" Ken asked.

"I wanted to get Clint Adams to do it, but now he's gone," she said.

"How do you know that?"

"Finch wouldn't have come to see me if he wasn't."

"Do you want me to come with you?"

"No," she said, "I'll be fine."

"So with Adams gone everythin's comin' to a head, huh?" Ken asked.

"Yes, it is," she told him. "You just stay here. Do your job."

She left and headed for the Black and White Saloon.

Chapter Forty-Four

When the lady with the purple gloves entered the Black and White Saloon the new sheriff and his deputy were sitting at a table. They knew this couldn't be good news.

"What do we do?" the deputy asked.

"Be ready," Sheriff Holton said.

"I don't even have a badge," the deputy said.

"Just watch Byron," Sheriff Holton said, "and be ready."

***

Byron watched Minerva walk to the bar. He reached down and put his hand on his shotgun.

"I guess Finch is dead," he said.

"Yes," she said.

"And me?"

"We can make a deal."

"Partners?" he asked.

"I don't think so."

Byron looked over at the two new town lawmen as he closed his hand over the shotgun. Both men came to their feet, drawing their guns. Before they could clear leather, though, Clint stepped through the batwing doors, gun in hand.

He fired twice and both men were hit in the chest, Holton right beneath the badge. As they fell to the floor, Clint turned toward the bar.

"Hey wait," Byron said, pulling his hand away from the shotgun, "don't shoot!"

Clint held his fire, but Minerva drew her gun from her garter and shot Byron in the chest.

Clint approached the bar, reloading his gun, and asked, Minerva, "Why'd you do that?"

She tucked the gun back into her garter and said, "I just made a purchase. What are you doing here? I thought you left town."

"So did I . . ."

***

When Clint rode out of town he was convinced he had seen the last of Kennelworth. But the longer he rode, and thought, the more convinced he became that things in town were going to explode. He didn't get very far when he reined the Tobiano in to do some thinking. He decided then and there that he couldn't leave until it was all over. Either Finch or Minerva was going to come out on top, and since Finch had personally pinned a badge on a new sheriff, it seemed likely that he and his cousin would come out on top.

That meant the lady was as good as dead.

"Or so he thought . . .

***

Now he realized he had backed the wrong horse. Minarva Dawson was deadlier than he thought.

"What made you come back?" she asked him.

"I thought four against one was unfair."

"You mean because I'm a lady?"

"That's what I thought."

"I haven't been a lady for a long time," she told him.

"So what's going to happen in Kennelworth now?" Clint asked.

"Changes," she said. "Starting with a new name, a new mayor, and a new sheriff." She looked him in the eyes. "And since there'll be so many new things, I might even be willing to throw in a free poke."

"Free?"

She smiled and nodded.

"But first I'll have to get someone to clean up."

"You know what?" he said, after a moment, "I think I'll hit the trail."

Now Available!

AWARD-WINNING AUTHOR
ROBERT J. RANDISI (J.R. ROBERTS)

For more information
visit: www.SpeakingVolumes.us